THREE WEDDINGS
AND A BABY

THREE WEDDINGS AND A BABY

BY

FIONA HARPER

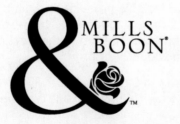

MILLS & BOON®

First published in Great Britain 2011
by Mills & Boon, an imprint of Harlequin (UK) Limited,
Large Print edition 2011
Eton House, 18-24 Paradise Road,
Richmond, Surrey TW9 1SR

© Fiona Harper 2011

ISBN: 978 0 263 22206 7

Harlequin (UK) policy is to use papers that are natural,
renewable and recyclable products and made from
wood grown in sustainable forests. The logging and
manufacturing process conform to the legal environmental
regulations of the country of origin.

Printed and bound in Great Britain
by CPI Antony Rowe, Chippenham, Wiltshire

For Joy,
a true friend with a big heart and open arms.

CHAPTER ONE

IF THERE was one thing Jennie Hunter had a gift for, it was getting away with blue murder. Unfortunately, her magical powers deserted her suddenly and unexpectedly one New Year's Day—around the same time a dishevelled arrangement of trumpet lilies and greenery hit her in the chest and then fell upside down into her waiting hands.

How had that happened?

She'd been actively retreating as her stepbrother's new bride had turned her back and hurled her bouquet over her shoulder into the waiting crowd. What had Alice done? Fitted it with a homing device? Jennie wouldn't have put it past her. Since she'd got engaged to Jennie's stepbrother she'd been trying to pair all her single friends off, and Jennie had become her pet project.

A damp, puffy hand clapped her on the shoulder. 'Don't worry, Jennie. It'll be your turn soon!'

She turned to give Cousin Bernie a smile that could probably have been more accurately described as a sneer. If he'd left a sweaty mark on her vintage satin bridesmaid's dress, she'd stuff this bouquet down his throat, petal by petal.

Your turn soon. How many times had she heard that today?

She looked down at the jumble of flowers and leaves in her hands, then turned it the right way up. Why had she clutched on to it when it had collided with her? Must have been a reflex. A whole herd of single women had been frothing at the mouth at the thought of securing this prize; she should have let one of them mow her down and scoop it up. As it was, she could feel their resentful eyes on her as the assembled wedding guests surged forward to say their farewells to the bride and groom before they got into their car.

Jennie was shoved along with the rest of the crowd, still holding the offending bouquet. There was nowhere handy to dispose of it, so she really didn't have much choice. She stood at the back of the crowd for a while, watching Cameron and Alice as they said their goodbyes, and even her current healthy dose of cynicism for 'true love' couldn't stop her sighing.

Alice looked gorgeous in her nineteen thirties vintage gown, like a willowy debutante. And Cameron? Well, he couldn't take his eyes off his new wife. And that was how it was supposed to be with newly-weds, wasn't it? The bride was supposed to be the centre of her groom's universe, his reason for living.

An unplanned scoffing sound escaped her lips. She disguised it as a cough and decided that this was as good a time as any to plunge through the crowd and say her farewells. Once she'd hugged her smug-looking stepbrother, she turned to Alice. The bride glanced down at the flowers in Jennie's hands and a satisfied gleam appeared in her eyes.

Jennie stifled another huff by stretching her lips wide. She held the bouquet up and did her very best to look pleased. Alice grinned back and pulled her into a hug.

'You deserve to find your special someone,' she whispered in Jennie's ear. 'Just wait until you meet him. He'll turn your world upside down and you'll be so happy you won't know what to do with yourself.'

What a pity Jennie had decided recently that she liked her world the right way up, thank you very much. Now, if only it would consent to *stay* that way.

She closed her eyes briefly, trying to mentally rearrange all the things recent events had turned on their heads. It took all her effort not to let out a giant sigh. However, by the time Alice released her, Jennie's eyes were open and full of the usual sass and sparkle everyone expected to see there. She was putting on an awfully good show.

And then the bride and groom were gone, accompanied by a flurry of confetti, shouts of good wishes and the rattle of tin cans. Their car sped up the curving drive of the exclusive country house hotel and Jennie felt all the air leave her lungs in one long *whoosh*.

Finally, it was over.

Now Alice and Cameron had left, people would just concentrate on drinking too much, catching up with long-lost relatives and dancing in a way they would regret when they found the inevitable videos uploaded onto FriendPages tomorrow.

Her plan was to find a quiet corner, kick off her heels and toast the death of her hopes and dreams with as much champagne as she could lay her hands on.

* * *

He watched as she turned and walked away—

No. Jennie Hunter didn't just walk. Walking was too ordinary a word. But he couldn't think of either a verb or an adjective that summed up the sideways sway of her hips, the elegant length of her stride as she crossed one foot in front of the other.

The bridal bouquet hung at her side, loose in her fingers, as she navigated the gravel driveway in heels. Other female guests picked their way across the uneven surface, but not Jennie. She didn't even look down, every step giving the impression she was gliding on a smooth and polished surface. Her ash blonde hair swung round her shoulders, just short enough to give him glimpses of a long and graceful neck.

A neck he'd suddenly discovered he would dearly like to wring.

Unfortunately, that wasn't an option. Not tonight, at least.

She joined a group of people and he could hear her laugh, clear and bright above all the others. She came alive at parties. Not surprising, since she'd made them her life's work. Being one of the most talked-about socialites on the London party scene had stood her in good stead when she'd started her own event-planning business. Everybody wanted to be at a party where Jennie Hunter was.

He sighed. Seeing her here confirmed all his worst fears and darkest thoughts about her. He so wanted to be wrong, but he suspected this wasn't a woman who could commit to anything for a month, let alone a lifetime. She'd fooled him. Maybe not on purpose, but he'd been duped, all the same. And that didn't sit easily with him. He was a man used to reading people in the blink of an eye, and he was rarely wrong. Why this woman? How had she managed to distract him from the truth?

He moved to get a better view of her as she approached the hotel entrance. Her recent lack of sociability had made her hard to find, but he'd known she'd planned to be at her stepbrother's wedding. Cameron Hunter had opted for a very private and exclusive affair. Friends and family had been sworn to secrecy, so it hadn't been easy to find out the exact location without causing suspicion, but he'd done it eventually.

He stepped out of the bush he'd been hiding in and straightened his tie. He hadn't crashed this wedding for nothing. Now the bride and groom had left, it was time to get what he'd come for. No, not revenge—although seeing her had started that beat pulsing inside his head—but the truth.

Who was Jennie Hunter? Who was she really?

When the last fluttering streamers of toilet paper tied to the back of Cameron's car had disappeared from view Jennie pivoted on her designer heels and headed back inside. Her arms went limp and the heavy bridal bouquet swung by her side, hooked loosely on a finger by its wide satin ribbon.

Suddenly she felt really tired. Exhausted. The smile she'd worn for Alice and Cameron as they'd driven into Happy Ever After started to fade. When she looked up and saw who was coming towards her the smile froze her features, making her face feel brittle.

Aunt Barbara swayed a little on her sensible heels. 'My favourite niece,' she announced loudly, the words bleeding into one another. She opened her arms wide and Jennie had no choice but to walk into the hug.

She was careful to extricate herself quickly and cleanly before her aunt's thick foundation left a smear on her dress. Secretly, she thought Auntie

Barb's penchant for orange-coloured make-up kept half her family's dry-cleaners in business.

'Come on,' she said gently, putting a steadying arm around the other woman's shoulders. 'Why don't we go and find Marion?'

Her stepmother was an expert at situations like these, always brimming with patience and grace that Jennie could only aspire to. She'd been the only mother-figure in Jennie's life for the last twelve years, and Jennie liked to think that they had the same sort of bond she'd have had with her own mother, if she'd lived long enough to see her daughter grow up. Well, *attempt* to grow up. There were some members of the family who had their doubts about that one.

Steering Auntie Barb through the smattering of guests who hadn't made their way back to the bar was harder than Jennie had anticipated. She scanned the crowd, desperate to locate the familiar serene features of her stepmother.

No luck. Just her father leaning on the reception desk in the lobby, waiting to talk to the clerk.

Auntie Barb turned to Jennie and squinted up at her. 'You're a good girl, really,' she said, patting her arm. 'And don't you mind—it'll be your turn soon, you mark my words.'

Okay. That was it.

One parent was as good as another, Jennie decided, as she altered course and headed straight for her father.

Auntie Barb erupted into movement and noise. 'Dennis!' She lunged at him and puckered up once more.

Jennie's mouth twisted into an off-centre smile. There was something very satisfying about seeing Dennis Hunter, president of Hunter Industries and ruler of all he surveyed, being engulfed in one of his sister's squashy orange hugs.

Jennie met his pleading eyes over the top of Auntie Barb's shoulders. *What have you done this time?* they said, but at least these days the familiar exasperated expression was tempered by an indulgent smile.

'Look who I found,' she said, making sure there was a twinkle in her eye as she delivered the words.

'Impossible child,' she heard her father mutter as her aunt lost interest in her one and only brother and turned to ask the reception clerk which way the bar was. The girl nodded in the direction of the pumping music and coloured lights emanating from the function room.

Her father swatted at a large orange smudge on his lapel with a handkerchief.

'I don't know how you managed to avoid it,' he said wearily. 'She gets me every single time.'

'It's a manoeuvre I've perfected over the years. Be nice to me and I might even teach it to you one day.'

Her father grunted. 'Oh, yes? And just how much will that set me back?'

'Nothing,' Jennie replied, and leaned forward to give him a kiss on the cheek, giving the orange smudge on his chest a wide berth. 'I told you the day I borrowed the start-up money for my business that it would be the last time I'd sponge off the old man.'

Her father gave another grunt. One of the I'll-believe-it-when-I-see-it variety, then he looked her up and down.

'I must say, despite my reservations about wearing second-hand stuff—'

'It's *vintage*. Like the stuff in your wine cellar. Supposed to get better as it gets older.' She batted her lashes and gave him her sweetest look. 'Just like you, Daddy.'

His mouth folded into a rueful smile. 'Impossible child.'

'You wouldn't have me any other way. Now…'
Jennie folded her arms and looked him straight
in the eye '…I had the strangest feeling you were
just about to pay me a backhanded compliment,
so you might as well spit it out.'

Her father coughed into his fist and shuffled
his feet. 'I was just going to say that I'm glad my
new daughter-in-law was so insistent about that
dress.'

Alice *had* been very determined to have her
own way on that matter. But since she and the
other bridesmaid, Coreen, ran a vintage clothing
business, there wasn't much Jennie could have
done to dissuade her.

This particular dress had been part of their
stock and Jennie had fallen in love with it the
moment she'd clapped eyes on it. And who
wouldn't have melted at the sight of the oyster-
coloured satin shift dress, cut to perfection. Pure
elegance. It fitted Jennie as if the dressmaker
had peered into the future and crafted it to her
exact measurements. She really shouldn't have
made such a fuss about it when she'd bought it,
because it had stuck in Alice's mind. And once
something was stuck in Alice's mind, it didn't
shake loose again easily.

So, when Alice had started making wedding plans, she'd started badgering Jennie about the dress. It was a crying shame to leave it sitting in the back of the wardrobe, apparently. Then Alice had gone on and on about a pair of shoes she'd once owned and how, when something was such a perfect fit, it just didn't do to chicken out of wearing it.

Jennie hadn't been about to tell Alice that, actually, she *had* worn the dress. Just once. And that, right now, she'd rather have worn a Bo-Peep monstrosity in polyester than put it on again. But that would have led to too many questions. Questions with answers she wasn't prepared to supply. So she'd worn the dress, and all day it had quietly mocked her.

He father coughed. 'I was just saying I think you look…that you're…'

That's about as expressive as her father got. Sometimes even back-handed compliments were just too hard for him to get out.

'What he's trying to say is that you look stunning.'

Jennie felt an arm curve around her waist and she turned to find her stepmother smiling at her, looking more relaxed than she'd been in weeks.

She'd pulled the whole wedding together in record time, because Cameron had been too impatient to wait any longer and had insisted he was marrying Alice the first day of the new year—starting it right, as he'd put it.

Marion broke eye contact and looked wistfully in the direction of the wide sweeping drive leading away from the hotel.

'They're going to be fabulously happy. You know that, don't you?' Jennie said and gave her a reassuring squeeze.

'Busted,' her stepmother replied, then gave a little laugh. 'That's the thing about being a parent… No matter how big and clever they get, you just can't stop them being the centre of your universe, can't switch off the internal radar that turned itself on the day they were born.'

That was all Jennie had wanted from her father after her mother had died—to know that she was even a little blip on his radar—but it had taken a couple of years to work out how to make herself shine brightly enough to get his undivided attention.

Marion sighed. 'It's so stupid. All I can think about is that we won't be seeing Cameron so often for Sunday lunch any more. It seems so selfish.'

Jennie rubbed her stepmother's arm. 'Nonsense,' she said, deciding to lighten the mood. 'I've tasted Alice's cooking, remember? I can guarantee you'll be seeing plenty of them.'

They both laughed, knowing they were supposed to, then her stepmother pulled away and turned to face her. 'And what about you? Are you "fabulously" happy, too?'

Jennie froze. She hadn't seen that coming, didn't know how to answer. Nobody ever asked her those kind of questions. They might ask her where she got those darling shoes from or who did her hair, but nothing that probed below the surface. Most people didn't think she was anything *but* surface. If little girls were supposed to be *sugar and spice and all things nice,* then when this little girl had filled out and grown up, all anyone had expected to see was *cocktails and fluff and all that stuff.* She'd been waiting for years for someone to ask more of her, to expect more of her.

Then one day, someone *had* looked deeper. Someone had decided to see if there was anything under all the fluff. She'd hoped there was, but his actions had spoken volumes on the matter.

She shook her head. She wasn't going to dwell on that—on him. And she didn't look for those kinds of questions now. Didn't want them.

'You're looking tired,' Marion said, frowning. 'What's the matter? You don't normally drift off like this unless there's a man involved somewhere along the line and you haven't been yourself since you got back from Mexico.' She left the inference hanging in the air.

Jennie shrugged and looked away. She didn't mention that, despite plans to holiday in Acapulco, she'd actually been in Paris. A last minute surprise. But telling her parents that would only make them curious.

'It was that stomach bug I got out there. Really took it out of me.'

'I'll say,' her father interjected. 'Hardly saw anything of you over Christmas.'

She folded her arms across her chest. 'Well, I'm all better now, so you can both stop fussing and checking up on me. Honestly!'

Her father chuckled. 'Don't you stick that bottom lip out at me, my girl. It used to work when you were eight, but it's well past its sell-by date.'

Jennie hadn't been aware she'd been doing anything in particular with her bottom lip, and she sucked it in and pressed the other on top of it. 'Better?' she mumbled through her closed mouth, with just a hint of a flounce in the way she threw back her shoulders.

'Much.' Her father did his best to give her a stern look, and failed.

Marion started to laugh gently. 'You're priceless, Jennie. One of a kind.'

Jennie frowned and hugged herself tighter. That was a compliment, right?

Her lips unsealed themselves, but nobody standing there had seriously expected them to remain shut for long, anyway. 'I don't see what's so funny. I just wish everyone would believe I'm all better now, no harm done.'

Seizing on the opportunity to deflect attention away from herself—who would have thought it?—she nodded in the direction of Auntie Barb. 'Which is more than I can say for some people.'

Marion graciously took the bait. 'Dennis? She can't possibly drive home. We're going to have to sort something out for her. See if you can do something, will you?'

'Humph,' was all her father said, but he turned and signalled to the girl behind the desk.

In the meantime, Marion greeted her sister-in-law and motioned for Jennie to help steer her towards a large sofa about ten feet away. A few moments later her father was back.

'No good,' he said. 'One of the reasons we chose this place was because it was small enough to book out for the night. They've confirmed we've filled it to the rafters.'

Jennie looked up the wide sweeping staircase. Perhaps she should just go straight to Plan B and slope off to her room? There was always room service if she decided she still needed bubbles to help her drown her sorrows.

'Bloody family,' her fathered mumbled.

Marion ignored him and turned to Jennie. 'Could we use your room? Just until we sort something out?'

They were interrupted by a not-so-gentle snore from the settee. Jennie's shoulders slumped. There went Plan B—up in flames.

'Of course,' she said, feeling her insides crumble, but standing straighter.

'Bless you,' her stepmother said and turned to gently shake Auntie Barb. 'It's not as if you'll be needing it for a while,' she said over her shoulder, and nodded towards the function room, from whence the low bass beat of an ABBA classic was thumping. 'The party's going to go on for hours yet.'

Whoopee. Another party. Just what she needed.

Her only option now was to hide in plain sight—sit herself at a table out of the way, preferably behind one of the large potted palms that dotted the room.

'Don't worry about us,' Marion said, giving her a little nudge in the direction of the banqueting hall. 'You go and have some fun. We'll sort Barbara out.'

'*Bloody* Barbara,' her father reminded. 'She always does this—refuses to "impose" on me by letting me pay for a room, then ends up having to stay anyway. Next time I'm insisting, and I don't care what she...'

Jennie tuned the rest of his rant out. Nothing for it now but to pull her features into her usual pixie-like grin and trot off like a good little party girl. And, after blowing her parents a kiss that ended in a little finger wave, that was exactly what she did.

He'd seen her glance towards the stairs and he'd hoped she'd let her feet follow her gaze. The last thing he wanted was to have this out in public, but the location would be up to her. He had no control over what she did next.

He almost let out a hollow laugh. No control whatsoever.

Look at him—reduced to skulking in bushes and crashing weddings just to have a few moments of her precious time. Something she was determined to deny him, it seemed. Well, just this once the spoiled princess was not going to get her own way.

He focused on her again, just in time to see her skip—actually skip—off in the direction of the party. Of course she would choose that over a quiet night in her room. She was Jennie Hunter. She had to go where she could be the centre of attention, where she could shine and glow.

A bitter taste filled his mouth and he swallowed. She really was unbelievable.

He'd been feeling calm and rational when he'd arrived, but all his composure had boiled away once he'd clapped eyes on her. Deep down, he knew he shouldn't confront her here, not when he was feeling like this, not in front of so many witnesses, but he couldn't stop himself following her.

He took the exact route he'd watched her take, her exit so imprinted on his memory he could foolishly imagine her shoe prints glowing subtly on the polished hardwood floor. Damn him for still seeing 'shine' where he wanted to see none.

However, there was not even a hint of a skip in his long strides as he entered the banqueting hall and began his search.

'Psst.'

Jennie spun round to find her fellow bridesmaid, Coreen, strategically sitting behind the last available potted palm.

Drat Cameron's generosity! The open bar, flowing with champagne cocktails, meant that, instead of trailing off into the night, most of the guests had returned to the reception to make sure her stepbrother got his money's worth. The room was heaving, and her fantasy of finding a quiet corner had already died. Now she was just hoping to find a seat.

Coreen parted the fronds of the palm and leaned forward. The effect of her nineteen-fifties pin-up looks surrounded by all that greenery really was comical, but Jennie couldn't bring herself to even muster a giggle. She waved back at Coreen, not even bothering to smile.

'I have a spare chair and two of *these*,' Coreen said, shoving an open bottle of champagne through the foliage. 'Care to join me?'

There *were* angels in heaven! Jennie let out a long breath. 'Now you're talking,' she replied and swiftly skirted the large terracotta urn to plonk herself in the last available seat in the room.

Coreen, as always, looked flawless. She took her business seriously, and Jennie had never seen her dress in a twenty-first century outfit. Today she had on a fifties prom dress in an icy pink that complemented Jennie's oyster shift dress.

Coreen slid an open bottle of champagne across the table towards her. Jennie's fingers closed around the rough foil at the neck. 'So what are we drinking to?' She paused. 'And please don't say "Happy Ever Afters"!'

Without waiting for an answer, she put the

bottle to her lips and swigged. She took a long gulp, wiped her mouth with the back of her hand and let the bottle land with a satisfying *thunk* on the table. When she glanced up, she found Coreen looking at her, a knowing smile on her sculpted lips.

'Wedding day blues, too, huh?'

'You have no idea,' Jennie said dryly and lifted the bottle again. Coreen, in the meantime, managed to attract the attention of a waiter, despite the fact he was being waved at from all over the banqueting hall. Well, maybe it wasn't *that* surprising. She was *Coreen,* after all. She signalled they'd like a couple of glasses and he saluted her, all the while giving her a saucy lopsided smile, then scuttled off to do her bidding. Coreen didn't turn round again until his rather fine backside had disappeared into the crowd.

'Me, too,' she said, after letting out a long sigh.

Jennie couldn't help but laugh. 'The wedding day blues don't seem to be putting you off your stride much.'

A wicked little smirk pulled at Coreen's lips, and then the corners of her mouth turned down. 'It's not the same, though, is it? Flirting's all

well and good, but on days like today, everyone's
gushing about love and promises and for ever. It
can make a girl decidedly—'

'Suicidal?' Jennie suggested.

'I was going to go with *single*, but your word
is…descriptive.'

The waiter returned to flirt some more with
Coreen. She accepted the glasses he proffered
and dismissed him with a wave of her hand and
a movie-queen smile. 'I've seen that look in a
man's eyes often enough to know *he* wasn't thinking about love and promises and for ever.'

Still, it didn't stop her glancing over her shoulder to get a second look at the retreating fine
backside. Jennie pulled a glass across the table
and filled it with bubbles.

'And you are thinking about that?'

'Maybe. I don't know.' Coreen held up her glass
so Jennie could fill it. 'You?'

Jennie opened her mouth to make some flip-
pant remark and found she couldn't speak. Her
vision blurred. To disguise what was happening,
she reached for her glass and knocked half the
contents back. The bubbles lodged like boulders
in her throat.

A few short weeks ago she'd believed in all

of it. Love and promises. Forever. But not now.
Maybe not ever again.

'Hey.' The soft word came from somewhere
near her right ear and she realised that the
fuzzy pink blur crouching beside her chair was
Coreen. Jennie willed her mouth to stop quiver-
ing, clamped her teeth shut. This time she used
the backs of her hands to wipe her cheeks.

Why now? Why, after lasting all day without
caving in, had she suddenly fallen to pieces? It
was really pathetic. Maybe it was the way she'd
seen Cameron look at Alice earlier on. She'd
compared it to what she'd thought she'd found
and realised it had all been a dream. A whirlwind. And the knowledge made her ache deep
inside, way beneath her muscles and bones.

'You never know,' Coreen said, keeping contact
by leaving a hand on Jennie's knee, but perching
back on her seat, 'we might even be able to trade
these dresses in for the real thing one day.'

But that just made Jennie cry all the harder,
until her nose felt bubbly and her throat was
hoarse.

The hand on her knee squeezed gently.
'Although, secretly, I've toyed with the idea

of wearing nothing at all when the fateful day arrives,' Coreen added.

And suddenly crying turned to hysteria. The tears still flowed, but her sides started to hurt and she clutched at Coreen, and Coreen clutched her just as hard back. Somewhere in the middle of the rib-hurting cackles, Jennie became aware of someone standing a few feet away, looking at her, but she was enjoying the much-needed rush of endorphins too much to pay attention to who it was.

Coreen fell silent and Jennie's unaccompanied giggles seemed overly loud and jarring. She gulped the last remnants of mirth down and wiped her eyes again, this time in a more ladylike fashion. Her eyelashes were clogged together on one side of her left eye, and she opened her eyes as wide as she could until the lashes untangled. It was only then that she focused on the ominously still figure in front of her.

Her mouth dropped open and every last bit of hilarity left her body, taking all the oxygen with it.

The man standing there was tall, impeccably dressed. His dark hair was cropped severely close, adding a hardness to his already angular features. But it was his eyes that took her hostage—a clear pale blue that could easily have been compared to the soft colour on the horizon on a hazy summer's day. Only, as they pinned her to her seat, they were as warm as an arctic breeze. She even shivered a little, gripped her arms across her middle.

'Jennie?' There was an uncharacteristic waver in Coreen's voice, and it sounded distant, slightly unreal. 'Do you know this guy?'

Jennie swallowed, and that one tiny motion seemed to get her functioning again. Her voice returned. It sounded warm, almost normal, when she spoke, which surprised her to no end. She didn't take her eyes off the man dominating her personal space.

'Coreen, this is… This is Alex Dangerfield.'

Alex nodded at Coreen, but he, too, didn't look away. Maybe he couldn't either. And it wasn't just her sight—every sense was locked on to him. But it had always been that way. Right from the very start.

'You know him, then?' Coreen sounded more than a little relieved.

And then he spoke in his low, rich voice and

it rumbled through her, sending tingles up the backs of Jennie's knees.

'She really ought to,' he said, not even a twitch of a smile softening the sarcastic tone. 'I'm her husband.'

CHAPTER TWO

COREEN, who had stood up some time after Alex's arrival, now sat abruptly back down in her chair. For a long time she just stared at him, and then she transferred her gaze to Jennie.

'Your…?' She trailed off, seemingly unable to utter the word *husband*.

Jennie knew exactly how she felt.

Coreen's eyes grew wide. 'Is this true?'

Jennie nodded. Unfortunately, it was. She'd have heartily liked to deny it, but Alex was the irritating sort of man who would undoubtedly produce a pristine marriage certificate from his inside pocket at an inconvenient moment like this. The thought infuriated her.

In his absence, her anger towards him had been muddled up with stupid yearnings, weighed down with grief and regrets, but now it sprang free, unpolluted and unfettered, and rose up from the pit of her stomach and clouded her eyes just as effectively as her earlier tears had done.

Now? Here? At Cameron's wedding?

What was he playing at?

She opened her mouth to ask him just that, but he cut her off by talking across her to Coreen.

'Now we've made the introductions, do you think I might have a private word with my wife?'

Jennie flinched as he said the last word. She didn't feel like his wife. Didn't feel like the centre of his universe.

Coreen regained some of her usual faultless composure where men were concerned. A glint in her eyes told Jennie she was ready to give Alex some of her legendary sass if he tried anything funny. 'I'm not leaving you alone with Jennie unless she says it's okay.'

Jennie almost laughed. If the situation were less dire, she'd have been the first to book a ringside seat for a face-off between Coreen and Alex. But then she glanced at her husband and she changed her mind. She'd never seen him like this—so cold, so…hostile. Maybe, if she'd seen this side of him during their whirlwind courtship she wouldn't have been stupid enough to say 'I do' quite so hastily.

After all he'd put her through, she certainly

didn't. Or, even if that wasn't quite true, she wanted it to be. So it almost counted.

'It's okay,' she told Coreen, and stood up. 'Alex and I... Well, we...'

'Have unfinished business,' he said.

We *are* unfinished business, she wanted to say as she tried to work out if this was all some weird hallucination, as the thump of the music filtered back into her consciousness and she became aware of other people in the room again. Lots of people. Reality felt just as strange and unconnected, too, she discovered.

But it struck her that as much as she wanted to grab Alex by the scruff of his neck and *make* him explain properly why having a honeymoon with his new bride hadn't been the top of his list of priorities, she didn't have that luxury at present.

She had to get Alex out of here. Now. Before her father and Marion appeared. Jennie glanced around the room, suddenly glad the party was still in full swing. It made it much easier to blend into the background—something that was normally her worst fear. If things had wound down by now there would have been far too many speculative glances, far too many itching ears.

And, as much as she hated the idea of being the obedient little wife, the only way she could see that happening was if she did what Alex wanted and had this 'private word' with him.

It was ironic that during their pitifully short marriage—record-breakingly short—she'd craved nothing more than *private* time with him.

'Shall we?' he said, and motioned for Jennie to walk ahead of him. He'd gestured towards the large double doors that led to the hotel foyer. Jennie gave a tight smile to Coreen, then strode through the packed dance floor, weaving nimbly round the miscellaneous dancers.

Nobody could find out who Alex was. The uproar it would cause would not only get her in a lot of hot water, but the family scandal would overshadow the whole day. Normally, she wasn't averse to stealing the limelight from just about anybody, and she knew quite well that hers were the antics everybody filed their social memories by.

Do you remember at Josh's christening when Jennie…? Or Barb's fiftieth when she…?

And that couldn't happen to Alice and Cameron's wedding day. If she caused a scene, nobody would remember how delicately beautiful

the bride had looked or how heartbreakingly romantic the groom's speech had been; they'd just
label the day as the one when Jennie and her
secret husband had given them a firework display
they'd never forget.

Thankfully, Alex was her polar opposite when
it came to hogging the spotlight, and she was
counting on him to want somewhere quiet and
civilised to say whatever he had to say.

They were almost at the doors now and she
glanced over her shoulder. Why, she wasn't sure.
She didn't need her eyes to check if Alex was following her; the prickles running up and down her
back confirmed he was close enough to reach out
and grab her if she was tempted to bolt. Which
she was. He was a very sensible man.

She quickly turned to stare straight ahead again.
There was a fire in his eyes that was anything but
sensible, and then she began to worry that she'd
read the whole situation wrong. He didn't look as
if he was on the verge of being quiet *or* civilised.
Perhaps it'd be a better plan to convince him to
meet her somewhere else in the morning, when
they were both in a better frame of mind.

Why was he here? Why now?

Scalding anger spiralled up inside her. What

gave him the right to come and capsize her life again? What more could he possibly want from her that he hadn't already taken?

As they reached the foyer, she could see it was virtually empty, populated only by a couple of tired-looking hotel employees and a guest she didn't recognize. Once they were through the double doors, she headed into a quiet nook, just under the shelter of the grand staircase, and turned to face Alex.

Despite her swift about-face, he didn't bump into her. Not quite. But he stopped perilously close, only millimetres away. The prickles running up and down her spine shifted accordingly, flowing round to the front of her body, then up her neck and into her cheeks, making every follicle on her head tense. It was like being jabbed all over by a thousand acupuncture needles—and nowhere near as relaxing.

She took a step backwards and asked the question that had been clanging around her head ever since he'd materialised out of nowhere in the function room. 'What are you doing here, Alex?'

He stood there, terrifyingly still, not even blinking. 'Jennie, you're my wife! Why would you think that I wouldn't come and find you?'

Hot, salty tears burned the back of Jennie's eyelids. This was what she'd wanted, what she'd prayed for—to hear those words in his deep, rumbling voice. When she'd run away from him, deep down in her subconscious, this was what she'd ached for. But it was only when he *hadn't* followed that she'd picked her emotions apart and realised it.

But it wasn't supposed to be like this.

In her tear-soaked daydreams he'd pulled her to him, pressed warm kisses to her face, whispered his devotion. In her dreams he'd never looked at her with such disdain. No, the words were right, but everything else was wrong, all wrong. And she couldn't let him see how weak it made her feel.

'Well, you found me.' She put her hands on her hips, raised just one eyebrow. If there was one thing Alex couldn't resist it was a challenge.

She hadn't thought it possible for him to be more of a foreboding presence towering over her, but in his stillness he hardened further and his eyes narrowed.

'I came for two reasons… There are things you

need to know and, frankly, I think you owe me an explanation.'

An explanation. *He* wanted an explanation?

Her jaw muscles squeezed themselves into knots. 'Is that all?'

She hated herself as she waited for his answer, knowing that a small part of her still wanted to hear him say he'd come for her, that he needed her. Those arctic-blue eyes looked her up and down.

'Possibly. I'm not sure yet.' From the look on his face, anyone would have thought he really didn't care.

Jennie's insides crumpled uncomfortably, as if she were a piece of paper that had been squashed into a ball and discarded. The only way she knew how to stop herself disintegrating was to unleash the rage she'd been nursing for the last few weeks.

'Go to hell!'

At that moment Jennie wished she hadn't been brought up so well, because she'd have dearly loved to wipe that condescending look off his face with a stinging slap, the kind that would probably have hurt her as much as it hurt him.

The satisfaction at seeing him lose his cool, just for a nanosecond, would be worth it.

She turned on her stilettos and strode off in the opposite direction, no destination in mind, just needing to get as far away from him as possible.

Two things happened at once—she heard her stepmother's disembodied voice coming from above her and a large hand shot out and shackled her wrist. Her skin burned against his as she tried to twist herself free.

Only one thought filled her mind—she wasn't ready for this. None of it. Which was strange, because all she'd wanted for the last few weeks was to see him. She'd fantasised about it so many times. At first, she'd dreamed about throwing her arms around him and showing him enthusiastically how much she'd missed him. After that, her imagination had turned more to stamping her foot and screaming. Lastly, she'd envisioned herself looking stunning and aloof as he grovelled for forgiveness. But now she realised she wasn't even close to being ready to see Alex. It was as if someone had reached a fist down inside of her and pulled her inside out. She needed time to put everything back in its proper place.

And she certainly wasn't ready for her family to find out. She could imagine the look in her father's eyes, the utter disappointment. Humiliation washed over her in a warm wave.

But Jennie knew how to pull herself together, knew how to suck all that negative energy in and turn it into something bright and glittering. It was what she did best—what people loved her for.

She looked up to see her stepmother descending the large oak staircase and, with great effort, flicked the inner switch that converted all the dross caking her insides into dazzling pure gold.

'There you are,' Marion said, her gaze wandering over Alex and then returning to Jennie. 'I was just coming to find you.'

There was an awkward moment when nobody looked anybody truly in the eye, then Marion noticed Alex's hand clamped around Jennie's wrist and what was left of her serene smile melted away. She looked back at Jennie, a question in her eyes. Jennie did her best to send back an SOS, tempted to bat it out in Morse code with her eyelashes. Marion's head didn't move, but Jennie saw her agreement in a tiny blink that only went halfway.

Marion stepped forward and offered a hand to Alex, the picture of a gracious hostess—apart from her pinprick pupils. 'I'm sorry, I know I should be able to put names to faces after all the poring over seating charts and guest lists I've done, but with a wedding this size it's been hard to keep track. Are you one of Alice's friends?'

Alex didn't react straight away, unwilling to release his grip on his runaway bride. It was the first time he'd had any physical contact with her in weeks, which certainly hadn't been what he'd been expecting when he'd booked a romantic honeymoon in Paris as a surprise for his bride-to-be.

He glanced at Jennie, at the open door at the other end of the hotel foyer, and reckoned he had a ninety-nine per cent chance of snaring her again if she bolted the minute he let go. With anyone else he'd have estimated a hundred per cent chance, but this was Jennie—a woman with a gift for the unpredictable.

How different it had been the last time he'd touched her, when he'd woken her and told her about the call that had lit up his mobile phone in the early hours of the morning, of the family emergency that was about to change his life for ever. She'd been warm and fuzzy with sleep, and she'd pulled him back to kiss him before he left and they'd said their goodbyes with the keen sense of desperation only newly-weds truly understood.

He peeled his hand from around Jennie's wrist and felt cool air fill his palm as she snatched her hand away.

He'd promised her he'd be back as soon as possible and, even though that had been much longer than either of them had anticipated, he'd kept his word. But she hadn't believed him.

That had stung. It had also pulled the loose end of a string of doubts that had been unravelling in him ever since. Surely, if his wife knew anything about him at all, she knew he was a man who kept his word, honoured his commitments. It was part of the reason he was here tracking her down.

While in his darkest moments he'd wanted to wash his hands and walk away from this whole mess, he couldn't do that. Or at least he wouldn't be able to do that with a clear conscience until he found out that there truly was no way forward. And, to do that, he needed to discover why Jennie had so little faith in him, and why she hadn't kept her side of the bargain.

He wasn't the only one who'd made promises. They both had. But it had seemed he'd picked a wife who'd struggled to keep them for much more than a week. Heat flashed behind his eyes, spiking through him. Why had she let him make the most life-altering, soul-wrenching promises a man could make to a woman if she didn't trust him to keep them?

'Marion Hunter,' the woman in front of him said, startling him a little.

Jennie had mentioned her stepmother a lot during their brief relationship, always with affection and respect. Marion's hand was delicate, but her shake was firm and Alex knew instantly that he liked her. She was no pushover, no matter how cultured and elegant she seemed.

He'd been so consumed with finding Jennie that he realised he hadn't thought about anything past that, his mind a carousel of all the imagined excuses she'd have for her abominable behaviour. He hadn't even considered what he'd say or do if he met a member of her family this evening, and that just wasn't like him—he always saw the big picture, always planned ahead.

What had she told them when she'd returned from her honeymoon on her own? Especially when she'd eloped to Las Vegas with a man they hadn't even met.

Marion Hunter scowled slightly as she slid her hand from his. He'd bet Jennie hadn't painted him in a flattering light. But that didn't matter. He didn't care about being the villain; he just wanted answers.

He'd been so caught up in his own thoughts he realised he hadn't even opened his mouth to speak, and now he rectified his lack of manners. 'Alex Dangerfield,' he said, with a hint of a smile in his eyes, even if it didn't reach his mouth. But Marion Hunter looked at him blankly, as if the name meant nothing to her, and he guessed that as the scowl lines on her forehead returned she was mentally scanning guest lists, seeking a match. He decided to help her out.

'Jennie's hu—'

'Half!' yelled Jennie beside him, suddenly springing into life. She was smiling brightly, and her outburst had been one of her usual exuberant declarations, but there had been a tinge of desperation in the tone, a hint of a squeak because she'd pitched it too high. Marion just looked puzzled.

'What I mean is…' She took a deep breath. 'Alex is my other half, my…my new…man,' she finished lamely, all the energy and life whooshing out of her like air out of a balloon. Then she grabbed his hand and squeezed it, attempted to mould herself to his rigid side.

'We had an argument, and I thought Alex wasn't going to be able to make it, but he did, and at first I was shocked, but now I'm so pleased—really pleased.'

And then she looked up at him, her eyes begging, and the truth hit Alex like one of those cartoon ten ton weights that always landed on the stooge's head and squashed him flat. Because that was what he was—Jennie's stooge.

She hadn't told them. Hadn't even thought to mention the trivial matter of finding someone to spend the rest of her life with. How stupid of him to have expected otherwise.

Any pleasure at meeting Jennie's stepmother evaporated in a blistering cloud of rage. That was all he was to his wife—an insignificant detail.

Well, he didn't care what her family thought, didn't care what hot water his presence here got her into. He wasn't going to waste any more time.

Ignoring her stepmother, he turned to Jennie. 'I need to talk to you. Now.'

Her eyes widened almost imperceptibly, and the fake smile she was wearing hollowed out.

'I...I...'

She was saved from answering by a staggering group of rowdy wedding guests spilling from the banqueting hall into the foyer. They crowded round Jennie and her stepmother, talking loudly about what a smashing wedding it had been, and how they were having the time of their lives. Jennie started to edge away, but he made sure he stuck right by her side. He wasn't going to even blink until he got her talking. Taking one's eyes off this woman for an instant was a mistake.

'It's not a good time,' she said, her eyes large and appealing. 'How about tomorrow? We can talk in the morning—when everyone has calmed down.'

He just looked at her. Did she think he was that much of a mug?

Marion had escaped the throng of well-wishers and closed the distance between them. 'Everything okay?' she said lightly, her eagle eyes missing nothing.

Jennie bit her lip and nodded furiously, but

he guessed her stepmother wasn't fooled for a second. She looked suspiciously at him and he returned her gaze, candour in his eyes. He didn't have anything to hide, did he? It was his shallow-hearted wife who needed to worry about bother-some things like the truth. Marion looked as if she wanted to interrogate him, and he was quite willing to allow her. Let the games begin.

'How long have you and Jennie known each other, then?' she said, making it sound as if this was just chit-chat, but her eyes never left his face.

Jennie held her breath and went rigid beside him.

'A few months,' he replied.

'And how did you meet?'

'Through my business,' Jennie said on an out-breath. 'Alex is a barrister, and I organised a garden party for his law firm at the end of the summer, and we…well, we hit it off straight away.'

Alex almost laughed. She made it sound so normal, so restrained. Yet their instant connec-tion had blind-sided him. He hadn't been able to get enough of her, hadn't been able to stop thinking about her, wanting her.

'You must have missed her when she flitted off on her impromptu holiday. She was gone for weeks.' Marion Hunter lifted one eyebrow as she tried to gauge his reaction to her question.

Alex just let his eyebrows mirror hers, a slight crooked smile curling his lips.

'Yes, it was awful,' Jennie said, words coming out so fast they were almost tripping over each other. 'But, you know, we phoned every day… texted…emailed…' She trailed off and looked at the floor.

Marion watched him carefully as Jennie babbled on, and when her stepdaughter fell silent she nodded gently. 'You must be the *stomach bug* I've heard so much about.'

Jennie was still holding Alex's hand and now she gripped it with a strength he hadn't realised she'd had.

'Apparently so,' he replied, catching on. One of the things he'd liked about Jennie was her creativity. He hadn't realised it extended to fibs, too.

Marion turned to Jennie. 'Well, it seems as if Mr Dangerfield here is right. You have some talking to do, I imagine, so I'll say my goodbyes and leave you to it.'

'Don't go!' Jennie said, a little too quickly, then recovered herself, lowering her tone and smoothing her dress down with her free hand. And then he felt her relax, breathe out. She continued slowly, the hint of a relieved smile in her voice. 'After all, it's too noisy here, and it isn't as if I've got a room to go to—Auntie Barb's in mine, snoring away loudly, I expect. And it's late.' She turned to face him. 'We'll just have to catch up in the morning after all,' she added, not even pretending to look crushed by the fact.

Marion shook her head. 'That's what I was coming to tell you. We've got you a room.'

Jennie's mouth sagged. 'That's impossible! They were all full up only an hour ago.'

'But there's one room we booked that isn't being used tonight, remember?' Marion said, looking very pleased with herself. 'Of course, you'll have to move the clothing rails and hair and make-up stuff into a corner, but it's a large suite—I'm sure you'll manage.'

Alex had been standing still, vaguely amused at the exchange between daughter and stepmother. It was quite refreshing to find things going his way, with very little toil on his part. He had the feeling that if he just stood here and let events

unfold around him, fate would be kind. He would
get his answers, and he'd get them tonight.

Jennie began to shake, right down to her fingertips. He could feel her hand trembling in his.

'You don't mean…?'

Marion winked at Alex, clearly having decided he was a *stomach bug* that Jennie needed a
second dose of, and he was unexpectedly glad to
have found an ally, someone who realised Jennie
shouldn't always be able to shimmy her way out
of difficult situations, that she had to learn to face
the consequences of her actions.

'Should have thought of it sooner,' she said
mildly. 'I'm sure Alice wouldn't mind, and it
seems a shame to let the room go to waste.' And
then she pressed a key with a large plastic tag on
it into Jennie's hand.

Jennie clamped her fingers around it as if it
were a hand grenade with the pin out. And then
the tension bled out of her and Alex knew he'd
won. Funnily enough, he was disappointed by
her reaction. He'd never known her admit defeat
so easily. Her bullheaded determination was one
of the things he loved about her.

Maybe he'd been wrong about her from the
start. They'd rushed headlong into things, too

caught up in the whirlwind that seemed to storm and crash around them when they were together. Unfortunately, he'd forgotten that, while whirlwinds were awesome displays of natural power, they were ultimately destructive. What a pity he hadn't realised that until he'd been picking through the wreckage of his marriage, wondering what had gone wrong and whether it was even worth collecting the debris to see if it could be put back together.

In the end, he'd decided that all he really knew about Jennie Hunter was that she was the one woman who'd fascinated him, captivated him. Ensnared him. And that she'd run away the first time the going had got tough.

'You know where it is, don't you, Jennie?' Marion said. 'After all, you got ready there this morning.'

Jennie nodded dully and started leading the way. Marion grabbed his arm as he passed her and leaned forward to whisper in his ear. 'Good luck,' she said, squeezing gently. 'She's hard work—but she's worth it.' And then she walked smoothly across the foyer and disappeared into the banqueting hall.

Alex followed Jennie up the large wooden

staircase. Not as closely as he had before, but close enough to watch those memorable curves move under the satin of that dress.

She had to be wearing *that* dress, didn't she?

Finally, they reached the top of the staircase and she led him down a corridor to a vast pair of double doors. Instead of opening the door, she just stood there, the key clutched in her closed left hand.

She wore no ring, he realised.

Slowly, he peeled her fingers away from the key's plastic tab, and when he'd reached the last one he stopped. He realised the reason for her hesitation now, shared a little of it himself, if he were honest.

In gold italic writing, on the moulded smooth plastic of the old-fashioned room key were two words: *Bridal Suite.*

CHAPTER THREE

ALEX was glad the sun was finally lowering itself behind the trees and rhododendrons, changing the neat lawn's wide stripes a dirty gold colour. Garden parties were, by definition, a daytime pursuit, and he'd soon be able to legitimately say his goodbyes. Inside his jacket pocket, his fingers traced the flat buttons of his mobile phone. He imagined sliding it open and dialling the number of the local cab company he'd programmed in earlier.

When his senior partner, Edward, had suggested this event to thank the staff and schmooze their most important contacts, Alex hadn't been slow in voicing his objections. The beginning of September wasn't really the perfect time for an outdoor event, was it? But Edward wasn't cutting his annual sailing trip in Barbados short for anyone, so September it had been.

Luckily, the fickle English summer had only

got into her stride around mid-August and had decided to linger awhile yet. The day had dawned bright and sunny and all afternoon a warm breeze had rippled the petals of the late roses in Edward's borders. But then Edward was an annoyingly lucky man.

Alex sighed and sipped his cold beer. He supposed it had been a good party. To be honest, he'd coasted through it, moving his mouth when he'd had to, smiling if he really must, but he hadn't retained a single fact about anyone he'd talked to. He couldn't even remember what he'd filled his plate with at the buffet table. Unless it was connected with work, it seemed details were beyond him these days.

He found a lone wicker chair in the corner of the lawn and waited for the crowds milling in and out of the vast conservatory, or under the rose-twined pergola, to thin. It would look bad if he was the first to disappear, but once others had started to drift off he could follow their lead. The last thing he wanted to do was stand out in this crowd. That would mean they would expect him to be brilliant and eloquent, dazzle them with stories of trials lost and won. And, while he had stories aplenty, he knew that the greyness inside him would invade the telling. So, while he kept his distance, he let them whisper about his aloofness, his distance. Better that than let them find out the brilliance, the eloquence, only happened when he set foot inside the Old Bailey.

He'd got used to this—sitting at the sidelines, watching everyone else have fun—and he knew it should bother him, but he couldn't muster the energy. He wasn't unhappy. And at least he knew what to expect from life. No drama. No nasty surprises. He'd had his fill of those. He knew some of his junior colleagues joked that, if attached to a heart monitor, he'd produce a monotonous line instead of peaks and valleys, but he didn't care about that either. They were young. They didn't understand that peaks were often overrated and valleys could sink below the threshold of what you could bear. Let them laugh.

The sky grew bluer and bluer, from peacock through to sapphire, but still the guests didn't diminish. If anything, there seemed to be more of them. When someone turned a switch somewhere, and the paths, shrubbery and whole pergola lit up with a million little white lights, everyone cheered. Blues music started to play, and people under the pergola started to dance. Alex just frowned.

Great. Trust Edward to have a garden party that turned into an all-night rave.

'Should have guessed I'd find you sulking out here on your own.'

He turned to see Edward's wife, Charity, smiling down at him. She'd been a trophy wife fifteen years ago, but Edward had certainly struck gold. Far from being a blonde airhead, Charity was an astute businesswoman herself now, and there was no one more elegant and poised. She was the sort of wife men in their position should have.

Mocking laughter filled the inside of his head. He silenced it by standing and giving Charity a soft kiss on the cheek.

'I'm not sulking.'

Charity just smiled. 'Edward's been asking for you. Some bigwig he wants you to impress. He's out on the terrace.' She pointed to a huddle of dark suits at the other edge of the garden.

Alex sighed and gave his partner's wife a little salute but, before he managed to set off in Edward's direction, she tugged at his sleeve.

'It's about time you let her go, Alex.'

She didn't need to mention a name.

He looked at Charity, her face soft with com-passion, and it made a nameless part inside him even colder. 'I don't seem to remember having any say in whether she came or went,' he said without expression.

'You know what I mean,' she replied, a glint of her inner strength appearing behind that soft-ness. 'It's been almost four years. You've got to forgive her and move on.'

Forgive her? Even if he knew how, he wasn't sure he wanted to.

He shrugged one shoulder and nodded, hoping that would be enough of an answer, and set off in the direction of the group of suits. At least he wouldn't have to talk about this kind of stuff with *them*.

Talking to the suits wasn't hard, either. They didn't want small talk; they wanted legal facts and arguments. Even so, when he'd done his bit, he extricated himself from the group as soon as possible and wandered away from the house, down the lit path to the patio under the large pergola. He kept going, weaving through the other guests, until he reached the far edge, leaned against a post and let his gaze follow the way the grass changed from artificial green to inky blue as the glow from the fairy lights diminished.

He stayed that way for minutes, until something happened behind him. He was never able afterwards to quantify exactly what it had been—whether the noise level and laughter had increased, or the lights had flickered brighter. He'd half-thought he'd sensed a soft warm breeze, like the memory of the afternoon's sunshine, but whatever it was, he'd turned round.

His eyes locked instantly on the woman in front of him. A jumble of images rolled over him, each in shocking high definition. Pale blonde hair, the colour of sand on a Highland beach. The graceful flick of a hand as she illustrated a story she was telling. A smile that just seemed to grow and grow and grow. The fairy lights above his head seemed to buzz louder in response to her presence.

Everywhere around her there was colour, life. And not just around her—it seemed to be coming from *inside* of her. That wasn't possible, was it? But he just had to look around him to see that something had happened. Suddenly, people were laughing more, dancing with more abandon.

She swayed along to a song as she laughed

briefly with someone who'd been trying hard to catch her attention, then moved on. And then he realised she was moving towards him, and he was standing as stiff as one of his golf clubs with his mouth slightly open. He tried to blink and failed.

She looked straight at him, and her smile lifted at one side. 'What's this?' she said, her voice soft and slightly husky. 'Someone not enjoying the party?'

Alex didn't know how it had happened, but suddenly he was inside the bubble of noise and colour that seemed to follow her everywhere. He felt different. Lighter. Stronger. As if he wanted to laugh, shout and sing all at once. And the electricity! Had he stepped on a loose wire? Because that was the only possible explanation for the warm buzzing feeling travelling all over him. At once he stopped resting on the post and stood up. And then he smiled back. Not the fake pulling of lips over teeth his colleagues normally saw him do. This one just crept over his mouth and expanded all on its own.

'Who told you that?' he said, then smiled even harder as he sensed a slight irregularity in the rhythm of her breathing. How he'd sensed it, he didn't know. He just had. He wasn't alone in this. She felt it, too.

Her smile was warm and sassy. Inviting. It made her pale pink lips practically irresistible. So Alex bent forward and tasted them. She didn't start or pull away. She just closed her eyes and met him.

A while later he began to hear things again, feel something other than her softness under his fingertips. He realised she had her arms wound around his neck and he had one hand pressing against her back and the other at the base of her throat. They were both slightly breathless, and it helped his sense of equilibrium to see she was just as dazed as he was.

They stayed like that for a few seconds, forehead to forehead. 'And to think someone told me you didn't like parties,' she said between breaths.

Alex just pulled her close and laughed, actually felt it rumbling through him like a sound wave. 'Hearsay,' he said and kissed her quickly, dragging his lips away before he got lost again. 'This is the best party I've ever been to.'

But she had other plans. She used the anchor of her hands to pull him close again, until he could feel her breath on his parted lips. And then it was all gone again. The lights, the roses, the whole flipping garden.

People began to stop dancing and began to whisper. Nudge each other in the sides and give each other knowing looks. But Alex didn't notice the lull in conversation or even sense the pairs of eyes turned his way. No more monotone lines for him. His pulse was drowning it all out with a steady and emphatic bump.

Alex's hand closed around Jennie's and he tugged at the plastic key tag, yet she couldn't seem to let it go. She was totally terrified, and it was pathetic.

Terrified of the look of disgust in his eyes, terrified of what he was about to say—of what he might *not* say. Terrified she still loved him as much as ever, that the all consuming chemistry they generated together would overwhelm her. That she'd turn around and give in. But she couldn't do that. She needed to take a stand and let him know that she was worth more than being second place in his affections. Taking the wide path that led to destruction was not an option this time. Pity, because she'd been down that road so many times she knew all the motels by name.

He was so close. Just the graze of his jacket cuff against her bare arm was enough to make her hyperventilate. She was tempted to close her eyes, wish the events of the last month away, pull him into the suite and continue the honeymoon that had been so rudely interrupted.

By him, remember. Don't give in. Look where it got you last time—a ring on your finger, yes, but your heart in pieces.

She let him ease the key from her clenched fingers and stepped sideways, out of proximity.

His fingers weren't shaking. He didn't seem to have any problems functioning normally, damn him. She let out a silent sigh. She'd always known, right from that first night, that Alex was a man who knew how to be steady, who knew how to keep control, but she'd never realised he could be this *cold*. But, then again, why would she have done? She'd been too busy basking in the heat of a passionate whirlwind romance. Who gave thought to winter when the sun shone?

Her father had always scolded her for jumping into things with both feet, and she'd steadily ignored his criticism, believing her *nothing ventured, nothing gained* philosophy got her where she wanted to go. She'd been dumbstruck when she'd realised the truth—that the flip side of her approach was *everything ventured, everything lost*. This was what happened when you made a mess so big nobody could sweep it under the rug for you.

Alex pushed the door open and, with an economical hand gesture, indicated she should enter ahead of him.

For a moment she just stared at the scene in front of her. She and Alice and Coreen had got ready in the suite this morning, and the evidence of the chaos was still in place. A hanging rail with empty garment bags stood off to one side and there were pots of make-up and a pair of abandoned hair straighteners on the coffee table, spoiling the romantic impact this room should have had. Thankfully.

She walked into the centre of the suite's living room and stood there, waiting for the click of the door. Dreading it. When it came, she flinched.

All she had to do now was turn around and face him. Yet she didn't move, suddenly couldn't take her eyes off the champagne bucket in the corner of the room. An unopened bottle remained there, surrounded with melted ice.

She heard him take a step—just one—towards her, and then there was silence.

What was wrong with the man? Did he think he'd be contaminated if he got any closer? She spun around to find him studying her closely, almost analytically.

'The last time I saw you in that dress, you were promising to stay by my side for ever.'

She crossed her arms across her middle, uncrossed them again. 'Believe me, if I could have worn anything else today, I would have. It wasn't my choice. Frankly, I can't wait to get out of it.'

And toss it out of the window, she silently added. Or burn it. It would make a very elegant bonfire.

Alex's eyebrows rose slightly and his mouth tilted into a sarcastic smile. 'Don't let me stop you.'

There was literally no breath left in her body to answer him with. She tried anyway. 'You… You're…'

'Insufferable? Judgemental? High-handed?' The smile twisted his face further, and he walked towards her. 'Heard it all before. I can keep going with adjectives until I come up with something more fitting, if you like.'

'I... You...'

His eyes narrowed. 'How about this for a description? *The man you deserted before the ink was dry on the marriage certificate?* I promise you, that's a brand new one for me.'

Jennie wanted to laugh, but it came out as a cough. What parallel dimension was this guy living in? She felt like punching him on the nose, and she bet that'd be a brand new experience for Mr Alex Dangerfield as well.

'*I* deserted *you?* That's rich!' She closed the rest of the distance between them, looked him right in the eye. 'Who was it exactly who sat on their own in a hotel room for almost a week after her new husband had vanished into thin air? Not you, that's for sure!'

'You're being ridiculous. I didn't *vanish,* as you call it. You knew where I was going and why. I phoned while I was away. And I distinctly remember apologizing and promising I'd be back. What more could I have said?'

The fact that he sounded all calm and reasonable had her consider throwing that punch. Unfortunately, just as her fury reached boiling point, it evaporated, condensing into moisture that stung the backs of her eyes.

It was all the things he *hadn't* said that had been the problem. For a few wonderful months, she'd been the sole recipient of all Alex's love, devotion and attention. And, with a man as intense as Alex, that was a heady cocktail. She'd felt lit up by him. When he looked at her, it was as if she was in the beam of a scorching bright searchlight but, instead of withering under its bleaching stare, she'd come alive, sparkled all the brighter. It was where she'd thought she was supposed to be. She hadn't cared if anyone else had paid her attention or not. All she had wanted to do was live her life in the warmth of Alex's spotlight.

Maybe she'd been out of her mind, drunk on that feeling, but all she knew now was that when *that* phone call had come, his light had swung away and focused somewhere else, and she'd been left shivering in the shadows, feeling lost and hungover.

In those short, hurried phone calls, often on car journeys between appointments, he'd given her information, but never reassurance. And then a trip that had only been supposed to last a day or two had dragged on and on…

'You never did properly explain what kept you back in England for so long.'

He opened his mouth to answer her, but she cut him off.

'I know that Becky was injured in a car crash. I'm not saying you shouldn't have gone, but I don't understand why it had to be you standing at her bedside. She divorced you. Where were her family? Couldn't they have visited her and fluffed up her pillows?'

'I would have explained if you'd given me a chance, but it's kind of hard to have a meaningful conversation with a dial tone!' He looked really angry. Jennie started to get scared, but then he breathed air out through his nose and looked at her more intently. 'She was my wife once, too, Jennie. And there are things you don't know. About my first marriage… About what I discovered when I got to the hospital…'

He straightened even further. 'When we split up, there was a lot that was left unsaid. When that phone call came and I knew her injuries were serious, that she'd asked for me, I had to give Becky the chance to say what she needed to say before it was too late. Surely, you can understand that?'

Jennie nodded, but it was a hollow gesture. She knew she should understand, but she didn't. How could she when Alex had mentioned an ex-wife, but had hardly said more than that? She'd thought his lack of communication on that matter had been because it was all done and dusted, in the past. Alex was like that. Once he closed the lid, walked away from something, he never went back to it. But, sitting in that hotel suite on her own, she'd started to come up with other reasons.

What if he'd never truly got over his ex-wife? What if he still loved her deep down? What if he'd realised, when he'd learned about the car accident, and he'd thought that his first wife was teetering on the edge of life, that everything he'd had with Jennie was just fluff and sparkle, that he had to drop everything to be with the first Mrs Dangerfield?

And, in those terse calls, Alex had done nothing to dispel those fears.

She looked at Alex now. Really looked at him. There was anger and frustration furrowed into his brow and his shoulders were bunched, but deep in his eyes there was something else. A weariness she'd never seen before. Hopelessness. Loss. While she feared what all that might mean, a part of her reached out to him, wanted to soothe him and make it all better.

Why hadn't she seen that the first moment he'd stood in front of her in the party? It wasn't as if she hadn't memorised every contour and plane of his face, the exact shade of the ring around his irises, the sharp line of his cheekbones and the tiny betraying lines at the corners of his eyes.

She'd been too focused on herself, on what *she* wanted, what *she* felt. Hadn't she been guilty of everything she'd just accused him of? She'd spent all that time in the hotel worrying about her feelings of abandonment, not worrying about Alex and all that he must have been going through. How selfish she'd been. Despite all her attempts to grow up and be a better person, she was just as shallow as ever.

She turned her ankle in on itself and rubbed the carpet with the toe of her shoe. Sudden and unusual insight hit her straight in the stomach. 'There's more to all of this than you told me, isn't there?' And she knew she wasn't talking about feelings for his ex-wife. It was bigger than that.

Alex looked slightly taken aback, though he

hid it well, but Jennie had seen the unmistakable flash of surprise in those pale blue eyes. He nodded.

'Becky died.'

All the air left Jennie's mouth, leaving her incapable of forming words. She'd died? Becky Dangerfield had died? She looked at Alex. He was watching her reaction, a hollow look in his eyes.

'Why didn't you tell me things had got that serious? She was making progress, you said...'

He looked away. Jennie hoped fervently it wasn't because he was too disgusted to look at her, but she couldn't blame him if he had.

'She was. But she took a sudden turn for the worse. There wasn't anything the doctors could do.'

'But...'

'I tried to tell you—' he said, flashing a look back in her direction. Yep. Disgust was clearly evident. Jennie felt sick. '—but you hung up on me and turned your phone off.'

She hung her head. Her quick temper was always getting her into trouble. But she'd been so cross! He'd been missing from their honeymoon for four days when he'd finally had the inclination to call her and talk to her for more than sixty seconds. She'd been looking forward to hearing his soft, sexy voice telling her she was all he could think about, that he couldn't spend a moment more away from her side... Fat chance. Alex had sounded all calm and matter-of-fact when he'd announced he wouldn't be coming back to Paris, that she needed to get herself on a train and be there at his side. He needed her. He had things to tell her.

It had been the last straw, confirming all her doubts about what sort of priority the first Mrs Dangerfield had in his life. At least, she'd *thought* it had confirmed all her doubts. The fact she'd been so wide of the mark made her feel even more queasy.

She'd packed her bags and left the hotel within the hour.

Oh, she felt so ashamed of herself. Her father was right. Her fling-herself-in-at-the-deep-end approach was nothing but foolishness. She'd hurt Alex horribly. She looked up at him. He wore a guarded expression and his lips were taut. Her stomach bottomed out further.

'That's not all, is it?' she asked, her voice wavering.

Alex shook his head again. 'I found out…something else…just before I called you that last time, but I didn't know how to—' He broke off and looked away. 'It was all so complicated. And I wasn't sure what was truth and what was fiction. Besides…it wasn't the sort of thing I could have told you over the phone.'

Big red alarm bells went off inside Jennie's head. 'Why?'

He looked away again, and his tiny admission of guilt hit her just as hard as the right hook she'd been contemplating landing on him a few moments earlier.

'You didn't trust me,' she said quietly, answering her own question.

Nobody ever trusted her with anything important. She was madcap Jennie—impulsive and wild, but tons of fun. And, even though she'd tried to shake that reputation in recent years, she'd gone and mucked it up by dropping everything, including her business commitments, and flitting off to Vegas to marry a man she'd only known for a few months.

'No,' Alex said, all hint of smiles, sarcastic or otherwise, gone. 'Don't you dare accuse me of that. It was you who didn't trust me. You didn't believe me when I told you that I'd get back as soon as I could.' By the time he'd finished talking, his voice had gone from low to almost shouting.

Jennie matched his volume. 'It was our *honeymoon,* Alex! Funnily enough, I expected you to actually be there!'

His jaw clenched and the next words came out with difficulty. 'I did get there.'

She sat down suddenly, landing in a large armchair. 'You did?'

He'd come for her? Come after her?

Her stomach rolled and she cupped a hand over her mouth. How could that be true? She would have known. A week after their Las Vegas quickie wedding they'd flown to Paris, but the following night that phone call had come, and early next morning Alex had boarded Eurostar and travelled back to London, assuring her he'd be back within twenty-four hours. And then it had started—the pacing round the hotel suite, the staring at the phone on the bedside table.

In those few short days inside the hotel room, everything had become magnified—the sense of loss, the fear he'd never come back again, the creeping feeling that things would never be the same. Thinking back now, that time had a simi-lar...*flavour*...to the weeks after her mother had died. The sense of confusion had been the same. And, just as her father had been after her mother's funeral, Alex had seemed hidden behind a brick wall that she hadn't been able to scale.

Leaving the hotel in Paris had been a desperate act, not a logical decision. At that moment she'd truly believed her marriage to be crumbling. If only she'd been patient—grown-up—about Alex's absence. If only she hadn't let panic make her decisions for her. She'd been so stupid.

She had come back to England, just as Alex had asked, but she hadn't remained in London. Well, only long enough to delete all of Alex's puzzled messages from her answer phone with one furious press of a button, then pack a small case.

She hadn't even told her family she was back—they had still been under the impression she was sunning herself in Mexico. That had suited her just fine. She'd needed time to lick her wounds before she was ready to face anyone—especially Alex—again, so she'd hidden out for more than a week in a little cottage on the Norfolk coast that a friend owned. After that she'd gone back to her flat. But her answer phone had been silent that time. And the voicemails had stopped arriving on her mobile in the middle of her week away. Even though she hadn't known where Alex was at that point, his apathy had radiated in waves across London. So, too ashamed to admit her most spectacular 'scrape' yet to her family, she'd kept quiet, hopped back into her life with a smile on her face as if nothing had happened and had tried to work out what to do next.

Her conscience had prickled her, telling her to call him instead, but she'd been too hurt, and hurt had quickly hardened into pig-headedness. She hadn't *wanted* to be the bigger person. In her mind, it had been up to Alex to make the first move, to prove with his actions that he still wanted her, because if she hadn't been first place in his life, what was the point of continuing with their marriage?

She'd wanted to believe that Alex had intended to return to her in Paris. She wanted to believe him now, but he was wrong: she *had* trusted him, but she didn't want his pity or false assurances now. And she wasn't ready to let him humiliate her a second time. So, instead of falling into his arms, she crossed her legs, stretched her arms across the back of the chair and gave him a tight smile.

'You finally deigned to show up? That was big of you.'

Alex ignored her childish comment, which just made her want to goad him all the more.

'When I finally arrived at the hotel,' he said, 'they told me my bride had checked out two days earlier.'

Jennie didn't react. What did he expect? They'd been married for just over a week when he'd disappeared. *A week!* What woman wouldn't have taken that as a major hint? Oh, no, there was no way she was letting him play the part of 'victim' in this scenario. That job was hers and she was going to milk it for everything it was worth, make him pay for discarding her so easily.

'Okay, Alex. Put your money where your mouth is.' She raised her eyebrows. 'If you actually do trust me, if I'm the one who's totally in the wrong, tell me now. What really happened between you leaving me in Paris and coming back to find me? What else do you need to tell me?'

Alex inhaled quickly and exhaled slowly.

Carefully, deliberately, he cleared the coffee table of make-up and other wedding preparation debris and then sat on the edge, facing her, elbows propped on knees, hands clasped together.

'I know I need to explain. That's part of why I'm here now.' He paused and his knuckles paled. 'But I'm not sure you're going to like what I've got to say, and I'm not sure you'll want to stay married to me when you know the truth. It'll change everything for us—all our plans, how we pictured our lives together.'

Jennie swallowed. He sounded so serious she was halfway to regretting her flounce back across the Channel in a fit of pique. But it was obvious he didn't understand her at all. She always flung herself into her adventures with everything she had, and she'd meant to approach her marriage the same way—one hundred per cent commitment, one hundred per cent loyalty. It had smarted when she'd believed that devotion hadn't been returned.

She rolled her lips in on themselves, moistening them. 'Do you… Do you even *want* to stay married to me?'

Alex didn't move, but his eyes suddenly grew hollow with despair, changing his whole expression. Jennie's heart did an irregular little beat.

'When I make promises, I keep them,' he said.

CHAPTER FOUR

HE'D spoken the truth—he didn't go back on his word, even if it cost him. Bailing out of things because they were too difficult was weak.

He looked at Jennie, sitting in the chair opposite him, her mascara-laden eyelashes blinking back moisture, and suddenly he felt ashamed of his behaviour. When he'd come up the hotel drive earlier that evening, he'd been in control of himself, remembering all the reasons why he needed to find Jennie and talk to her, but the minute he'd seen her all his noble intentions had skittered away.

What was it about her that fried all his senses? Really? Nobody else ever had this effect on him. He managed to walk down the street, hold down a good job—basically, live his life—without losing control of his emotions, so how did one woman overturn all that?

Right. From this moment on, he was going to

pull it all back and start behaving like an adult. It wouldn't be that hard. He only had to think of the look of raw vulnerability in his wife's eyes when she'd asked, her voice wavering, if he wanted to stay married to her. It had pierced him, and all his anger had drained out of that tiny hole in an instant. He'd felt something pure, something real. Something that had hitherto been suffocated by his self-righteousness, and it had him questioning every prejudice he'd had about her.

It was as if there were two Jennies—the one he'd married and the one who'd deserted him— flickering in and out of sync with each other, like the deteriorating picture on an old TV set. But which one was real and which one was the mirage?

The woman he'd fallen in love with had been vivacious and intelligent and capable, a woman who took everything life threw at her in her stride. He'd respected her strength, her bravado, but maybe he'd been blinded, as the old saying suggested. He'd thought her resilience had come from inner strength, but after she'd left Paris he'd considered that maybe there was another explanation. Perhaps the strength he'd ascribed her had just been shallowness. Maybe it had been that, apart from herself, nothing really mattered to her and, therefore, she couldn't be wounded by anything.

He'd lived through hell for the five days he'd been away from her, and had watched a woman he'd once loved wither away in a hospital bed until someone had asked him for a decision to turn the switch off. He'd still been named her next of kin, and none of her scavenging family had been found to dispute that. But it was only after that that things had got *really* complicated. He'd needed Jennie—needed her to be her bright, bubbly, affectionate self, needed her to hold him together when he'd thought he'd been about to fall apart. The fact that she'd had a tantrum and stomped off home like a spoilt princess hadn't gone down well at all.

After his wasted trip to Paris to find his missing bride—hours he could have spent much more productively—he'd come back to England exhausted, and had been thrust headlong back into the horrific consequences of his ex-wife's death. One surprise had come after another as the four years since he'd last seen her had slowly unravelled themselves before him and given up their secrets. Just as well he did what he did for a living and that where his expertise wasn't relevant, he had friends and contacts who could point him in the right direction.

And in his spare time he'd tried to find his new wife. He'd called her office, her home, her parents' home, but the story had always been the same: Jennie was on an impromptu holiday, having the time of her life. At first he'd wondered if they'd all been stonewalling him, but after meeting Marion Hunter earlier this evening he'd got the feeling that her family had been just as much in the dark as he had.

Eventually, he'd given up. Waited for her to stop ignoring his calls and come to her senses. Christmas had arrived soon after that, and he'd decided to wait for her stepbrother's wedding to confront her. He had family who actually wanted to be around him, and life-changing news to break to them. Tired of searching for a wife who didn't want to be found, he'd concentrated on that for a few days, knowing the inevitable showdown would happen soon enough.

He looked at her. She had been relaxing in the armchair, but now she was leaning forward, her eyes large, all traces of her sassy smile gone, and it gave him a terrible sense of déjà vu. Right now she looked very much like the woman he'd married. Which was very confusing, because he wasn't even sure if that woman was real.

But…if the Jennie he'd married wasn't a mirage, he might have to label her differently. Could he? Could he rip off the one saying 'problem' and replace it with one that read 'solution'? Did he trust her enough to even find out?

He needed time to think, and created some by walking over to the champagne bucket and hoisting out the dripping bottle. He held it up and asked Jennie a question with a tilt of his head.

'If there was ever a time I needed a drink,' Jennie said wearily, 'it's now.' She nodded at a tray of clean glasses on the sideboard nearby, and he took his time opening the bottle and filling them. When he was ready, he handed her a glass and sat down on the sofa opposite her.

To find out the truth, he was going to have to excuse himself as prosecutor, a role he seemed to have slipped into without realising it, and remind himself he was supposed to treat what he heard, not even as if he were an impartial judge, but as if he were a jury member. He had to hear what she had to say expecting only truth and innocence, convicting her mentally of no crime until all the evidence was in, even if the events of the last couple of weeks screamed at him to do otherwise.

So he leaned forward and looked her in the eye. They both had questions that needed answering, but he had to remember not to goad and trap as he usually did during cross-examination. These days he had enough seniority in his chambers to pick and choose his cases, and he no longer immersed himself in defence work, as he'd done when he'd been married to Becky and had believed that every underdog had deserved its day in court. Nowadays, he only took prosecution cases if he could help it. Protecting those who couldn't protect themselves also involved punishing those who preyed on them. But he'd got used to being suspicious, of seeing the lies everyone tried to hide behind. He'd have to snap out of it now and act as if he were conducting a defence—gently guide her, lead her and hope she'd give the right answer on cue. It wasn't so long since he'd last done that. Surely he could remember how?

He kept his voice low, coaxing. 'I know you were upset when I asked you to join me in London, but why did you disappear? Why didn't you come home?'

'Men,' she muttered. 'They never understand anything.'

'Explain it to me, then.'

Jennie stared at him for a few seconds, then took a big gulp of her champagne. 'You have to understand, Alex. Spending days on my own, pacing round a hotel room only to slope off back to London without my groom wasn't exactly the fairy tale I'd pictured when I'd imagined my honeymoon.'

He knew that. Of course he knew that. But it had been an emergency. Something he hadn't asked for and hadn't been able to control. What else could he have done? It had broken his heart to phone her and tell her there was no way he could come back yet, that they'd have to postpone the rest of their trip. There were things he needed to tell her—things he'd really needed to say in person, not over a dodgy mobile connection.

'I know,' he said. 'It wasn't how I wanted it, either.'

He could imagine how disappointed Jennie had been, how much the reality had differed from her fairy tale. His reality hadn't been any rosier, and there were memories from that time he wished he could wipe from his consciousness: Becky, grey and lifeless in a hospital bed. The awful silence after the life support machine had been switched off, much worse than the hiss of the ventilator or the increasingly regular alarms. The clawing sense of regret over how things might have been different, if only she'd let him help her.

'I thought I'd done the best I could, given the circumstances, Jennie. I didn't have much choice. If it hadn't been important, I wouldn't have asked it of you.'

Jennie made a strange little laugh under her breath. 'My father used to give me that excuse all the time,' she said forlornly, then she dropped her voice to a low rumble. '"Not now, Jennie. This is important!"' She finished her impression and gave him a smile that wasn't in the least convincing, then began talking too fast and endlessly creasing the stiff bow on the front of her dress. 'I didn't think I'd ever hear that excuse from you. It took me by surprise. Normally, if I know that kind of thing's coming, I can prepare myself, cushion myself against it… But with you, there was no warning! I just… I didn't…'

He didn't say anything. His mind was too busy stretching to accommodate the flurry of words.

'You want to know why I didn't race to your side the moment I left Paris?'

He nodded. Of course he did.

Jennie pursed her lips, then nodded back at him. 'Well, I needed time. And I supposed you needed time, too.'

Time for what?

'To decide what you really wanted,' she added, but he couldn't shake the feeling that she'd switched a word at the last moment. Not *what,* but *who. Who* you really wanted. And suddenly he started calculating mentally, adding up hours and minutes, doing the kind of maths Jennie must have done.

The clock had never been anything but a way of carving up the day to Alex. He hadn't realised that seconds could be as precious as gold, to be hoarded when others spent them on you, or to be considered stolen if bestowed elsewhere. His absence hadn't just been an inconvenience to Jennie, as he'd imagined. To her, it had been a gauge of his love.

She let out a long breath and relaxed back into the chair cushions again. 'I left because I thought—' she broke off to look back at him briefly '—that finding Becky again meant that you had decided...'

She didn't finish the sentence, just looked in her lap.

That just didn't make sense. Becky hadn't even woken up the whole time he'd been there with her. Jennie couldn't possibly think he actually... Any feelings he'd had for Becky had been those of sadness at a life wasted.

As far as he knew, he was the only person who'd ever given a damn about Becky, who had ever put her welfare first. Not even her family had given her that luxury. How could he have walked away and left her last moments to the hands of strangers?

Jennie was whispering now. 'The longer you were away, the shorter the calls became, the more distant you were. I didn't want to think it, but the old proverb's right, Alex. Actions speak louder than words, and it was pretty clear where your loyalties lay. Even when she'd gone, it was her you wanted to be with.'

The rage he'd tucked neatly away surged up his throat, stinging as it went. How could she think that? Hadn't the heady months they'd been together, all the promises they'd exchanged, been enough? Didn't she know him at all?

She refused to meet his gaze. 'I know we told each other we weren't rushing into things, that we knew what we were doing, but I started to wonder…if maybe you realised you'd made a mistake, that I wasn't the one you wanted.'

He closed his eyes. He'd hit the nail on the head. She really *didn't* know him if she thought he was capable of being that fickle, if she thought he could make those promises one week and then take them back, like unwanted gifts, the next. He just wasn't like that. And he had a wardrobe full of ghastly Christmas jumpers he never wore to prove the point.

But her reaction, while not particularly logical, had at least been honest. For days now he'd been worried about exactly the same thing. He'd wondered whether her departure was a sign that marrying him had been a whim, an impulse she'd regretted. He was relieved, he realised. Relieved that she'd left Paris because she'd been hurt, because she really *did* care, not because she didn't give a hoot.

Just knowing that turned everything he'd been stewing over on its head. Something liquid and warm flowed inside him, something he thought had hardened into anger and disappointment. He wasn't sure he wanted to feel it, but feel it he did, and he couldn't help the next words that left his mouth.

'That's not true, Jennie. Of course I wanted you.'

He heard the little gasp in the back of her throat. She blinked furiously and then her lip wobbled. All her bravado drained away, leaving her looking young and very fragile. In his imagination he could see her leaving the hotel in Paris—large dark glasses covering her swollen pink eyes, refusing to look back as the taxi pulled away because it would be too painful.

'I'm sorry,' he said simply. 'I didn't realise you felt that way.'

Now the tears spilled over and coursed down her face, but she didn't make a sound.

'Thank you,' she said in between sniffs, and went to fetch a tissue from a box on the small table. She sat back down and blew her nose loudly. 'I appreciate you saying that—but it's not enough. I need to know *why,* Alex. Why was she more important to you than I was?'

* * *

There. She'd said it, turned the fear that had been hiding round a corner in her heart into sounds and syllables. For a large chunk of her life, the people who mattered most to her had had more important things than her to tend to. She hadn't been neglected, after all. She'd wanted for nothing, been to the best schools, had everything handed to her on a silver platter. And she'd seemed happy enough. Why would anyone have thought she'd needed anything more?

Jennie realised that this was the first time she'd ever had the courage to ask why. Why were other things, other people, always more important than her? Her normal tactic in this kind of situation had been to persuade her loved ones to move her up their list of priorities by being the most dazzling creature possible. And if that hadn't worked, she'd got just naughty enough to bump herself up to the number one slot.

It was odd. She thought that if she'd ever let the words out to match what she felt, she'd crumple under the weight of them, but it wasn't like that. She felt strangely light, almost ready to hear his answer—no matter what it was.

She met his gaze.

He didn't blink, just pulled his shoulders back

and heaved in some air. He kept his eyes on her as he stood up and walked round the coffee table to sit opposite her on the sofa. This obviously wasn't going to be a quick chat.

'The history Becky and I had… It's complicated.'

She raised her eyebrows and mirrored his own response back to him. 'Explain it to me, then.'

His eyes glazed slightly, and she guessed he was cataloguing memories, trying to find the best place to start. Knowing Alex's ordered brain, he'd start at the beginning, lay a foundation, before he got on to the juicy stuff. She almost wanted to tell him to forget all of that, to put her out of her misery. There was a shift in his features, and she knew he'd found his 'in'.

'I grew up in a happy home,' he said.

Okay, if they were going to go that far back, this was going to take all night. She didn't say that, though.

'My parents wanted more children after they had me and my brother, but it just wasn't to be… By the time I'd started at university and Chris was studying for his A levels, I think my mother looked at her rapidly shrinking nest and decided to do something about it. So Mum and Dad decided to foster.'

She sat up straighter. He'd never mentioned that before, even though she'd heard plenty of stories about the happy-go-lucky Chris.

'What has this got to do with your first—' she couldn't quite bring herself to use the same title she now occupied '—with Becky?'

He took a moment before he carried on. 'Initially, my parents offered emergency foster care—children who needed a safe place to stay immediately, until they could be found something more permanent—but then they were asked to consider taking in a teenage girl.'

Her jaw loosened slightly. 'You mean that girl was…'

He nodded. 'I was away at university most of the time she was there, but slowly I got to know her. I can still picture her now, the way she looked the first day I met her. She was sitting in my parents' kitchen, drinking lemonade. Fifteen years old, but nothing like the girls I'd known at that age. Dressed as if she was about to walk the streets, but so thin her tight skirt was baggy and shapeless. She looked frightened out of her wits, as if she'd run if I made any sudden move.'

Jennie could imagine it. A feral young woman, twitchy and skittish, large eyes with huge dark circles underneath. And in her mind's eye she could see a young Alex, wanting to reach out to the girl to save her from all the awful things that had happened to her. Because that was what Alex was like, that was why he did the job he did. He felt the need to make things right, to protect people.

She tried hard not to listen to the question ringing in her ears, the one that prodded her to think about why he hadn't felt that same need to shield his new wife, why he had left her to cope on her own.

Thankfully, Alex distracted her with the rest of Becky's story. He didn't think much of his ex's family, that was for sure. From what he told her, the whole lot of them—father, mother, two older brothers—were all petty criminals, and had been in and out of prison more times than Becky had been able to count.

Jennie tried to sit back and listen to the story impassively, tried not to get emotionally involved, but the tale of a child whose only value had been as a lookout when a corner shop was being robbed or as a mule to carry anything her relatives didn't want to be caught with if the police turned up, touched her heart.

'Her father was already doing time when her mother was remanded in custody for cheque fraud,' Alex said. 'Becky wasn't immediately taken into care because she had older brothers who could act as guardians, but they didn't stick around for long. She tried to manage on her own for a few weeks but eventually she ended up at my parents' house.'

'That's awful,' she said, leaning forward.

At least her own father had tried to do the right thing after her mother died. It hadn't been his fault that he hadn't been able to connect emotionally with a sad little girl. It was the way he had been brought up himself—stiff upper lip, none of that sissy talk about feelings. Those were the kind of things his generation left to the women.

But poor Becky. She'd had no one. Not one person on her side—until Alex and his family had come along. Suddenly Jennie felt incredibly proud of the young man her husband had once been, proud of him for looking deeper where others had probably only seen a troublemaker.

'That's not the worst of it,' he said grimly. 'She had followed the only example she'd ever had to deal with the chaos in her life. By the time she came to my parents', she was recovering from a drug problem. At fifteen!' He shook his head. 'She wouldn't talk about some periods of her life at all, but once I'd qualified I filled in the blanks. I met many, many people like her father and her brothers over the years. I've heard stories that would make your hair stand on end…truly.'

She asked another soft question, urging him on, glad that he hadn't noticed that she'd turned the tables and that it was she who was cross-examining him. There was a heartbreaking look in his eyes—one she had yet to define—and she wondered if he was letting her do this because it felt good to finally say some of these things out loud.

He started to tell her how, over the next few years, Becky had fought hard to turn her life around. With the love and support of Alex's parents, she'd beaten her addiction, started going to school again. He didn't have to tell Jennie why he'd fallen in love with Becky, she could see it in his eyes. Despite her awful background, Becky had shown inner substance and strength. It was clear Alex had admired her for that and admiration had gradually blossomed into love. And it was hardly surprising he'd rushed to Becky's side when he'd heard she'd been injured.

Jennie tried not to make comparisons, but it was impossible and, with each word that Alex spoke, her mood sank lower and lower. His new wife had grown up with all the privileges a girl could ask for and what had she achieved, how much inner substance had *she* shown? Not much. It had taken her until the grand old age of thirty to work up the guts to stop living off her father and strike out on her own.

No wonder nobody respected her. She'd made her teenage years stretch way into her twenties, and nobody had expected her to do much with her life except be a drain on her daddy's platinum card. And, while she was starting to prove them wrong, she'd discovered that it took a lot more than a few happy clients and some money of her own in the bank to change people's opinions. In her family's eyes—and probably those of most of the people she knew—she was the leopard whose spots were well and truly tattooed on.

She drained her glass and filled it again from the open bottle on the coffee table. It probably wasn't a good idea, seeing as she'd never quite made it to the buffet table this evening, but she reckoned she needed a little extra fortitude if she was going to have to sit through the details of Alex and Becky's perfect first love.

It didn't last...a nasty little voice crooned inside her head.

She couldn't take solace in that either, though, because Alex had once let it slip that it had been Becky who'd done the leaving. Jennie knew the only way forward for her and Alex was to listen to what he had to say next, but she wished she could cover her ears. She didn't want to know how heartbroken he'd been when Becky had left him, or how many years it had taken to get over her.

What if it was more than four? That was how long they'd been apart.

She looked at Alex, watching her intently from the sofa, and felt an internal hiccup that never quite made it to the surface. The look in his eyes said there was much more to tell, and she was starting to think that what he'd said earlier would be proved true—that she wouldn't want to hear any of it.

CHAPTER FIVE

ALEX stared at the ceiling and tried to think how to condense the complex relationship he'd had with Becky into just a handful of sentences. He hadn't allowed himself to think about it for such a long time that it seemed like someone else's story, as if he was trying to summarise a film he'd seen at the cinema. If only this story could have been like that—flat and unreal, at a comfortable distance. Instead, his past was more like a juggernaut from an action movie car chase, but that juggernaut had come crashing out of the screen and into reality.

But there was no point getting emotional about it. He'd done his grieving, mourned the loss of his marriage already. What Jennie needed was information, and he was going to give it to her.

'We married young—too young, my parents said—while I was doing my post-graduate law degree. We both had to work hard to survive. It was a struggle, but Becky seemed to thrive on that. I can honestly say we were truly happy.'

Jennie suddenly stood up. 'I think I need some fresh air,' she said. 'Do you need fresh air? Let's open these windows.' Before he could answer, she was across the room and opening the glazed doors that led onto a small balcony. Instead of just opening them a crack, she flung one open and walked outside. He watched her for a moment, palms flat on the stone balustrade, arms stiff, inhaling deeply enough for him to see her back muscles move beneath the satin of her dress, and then he walked outside to join her.

It was freezing, but there was something about the chill in the air that re-energised him, got his blood pumping.

'Carry on,' she said, not looking at him, but staring out into the moonlit countryside.

He turned and rested on the balustrade and stared back into the warm room they'd just vacated. Then he kicked the door shut with his foot, guessing they wouldn't be out here long and they'd probably prefer the room to stay warm and welcoming.

'After I passed the Bar Vocational Course and did my pupillage, Edward offered me a tenancy at his chambers. It was a fantastic opportunity and Becky and I thought everything we had worked for had finally paid off.' He turned to look at Jennie, but she was still looking out over the moon-bathed downs. 'Success turned out to be a double-edged sword. In the first couple of years I did well on a few cases, started to make my name. Becky loved the lifestyle, the fact we could afford nice cars and that she could shop in exclusive boutiques instead of discount stores. We were able to move to a better area, and we started being invited to social functions connected with work, and in turn were expected to entertain my colleagues and clients.'

Jennie frowned and looked sideways at him. 'That sounds like a modern-day fairy tale, not a horror story.'

He nodded. At the time he'd thought so, too, but he'd been too pleased with himself, too infatuated with his own success to notice that Becky wasn't coping with being a barrister's wife.

'The hectic nature of Becky's life meant she hadn't got many qualifications, and she was suddenly thrust into a world of high-flyers and over-achievers and she struggled to fit in. But she'd seemed so happy and together for such a long time by then that I didn't realise just how many scars she still carried from her past.'

Jennie's gaze drifted down to her hands, splayed on the balustrade. He took her silence as an invitation to keep going.

'A few minor faux pas at some important functions only worsened matters. When she finally came to the end of her tether, she flung it all at me—how they all looked down on her, how alone she felt when I was always having to cancel nights out for a last minute meeting or was "obsessed" by a case for days, if not weeks, at a time.' He held a breath and then let it out slowly. 'After that she got really low. The doctor said she was suffering from depression.'

What he remembered most about that time, apart from the week-long silences, was the anger. The way Becky had looked at him as if he was something she'd scraped off the bottom of her shoe. Becky had blamed him. *He'd* put her in this situation. He'd wanted this life, so in her eyes it was all his fault.

And, yes, there'd been some blame to lay at his door, but not for doing what most people did. It was normal to want to make a success of yourself, to try to have a nice life. But he'd understood that Becky hadn't had much *normal* in her life. He'd tried to understand, tried to help the only way he'd known how.

'We got her help. We both went to counselling sessions. She saw a psychotherapist on her own… And for a while things seemed to get better.'

He stopped. Well, things had *seemed* better. Becky had been smiling again. He'd encouraged her to make new friends to widen her support system, and had been pleased when she'd taken his advice. He hadn't felt quite so guilty about all the times his job demanded he work into the evening or be away overnight. Okay, yes, he'd sensed an odd kind of distance between him and Becky, but he'd put it down to the aftermath of her breakdown. They'd even started trying for a family. He hadn't been sure they'd been ready for it, but Becky had seemed so set on the idea he'd gone along with it, hoping that having a baby to care for would give her something positive, something life-affirming to focus on. He'd known she'd make a good mother. Yes, she had her problems, but she had a heart of gold underneath.

At least, that was what he'd thought at the time. The things that had come to light after her death had put a huge question mark over that.

He'd never imagined she could be so cruel or so selfish.

'Alex?'

Jennie's soft question brought him back to the present. He stood up and opened the balcony door. She must be freezing. Jennie nodded and walked back inside, rubbing her arms with her hands. He wanted to offer her his jacket, but it felt too intimate a gesture—an imposition rather than a courtesy—so instead he picked up a chenille throw that he spotted draped over the back of one of the chairs and handed it to her. She draped it over her shoulders and sat herself back down in the same chair.

'But things obviously didn't *stay* better for you and Becky,' she said, looking at him from under the sweep of her side parting.

He couldn't quite bring himself to cosy back down on the sofa. He needed to walk, to think. 'No. Things got quite a lot worse.'

There must have been something in the hoarseness of his voice that got to her. While he'd been talking he'd got the impression that Jennie had been adding layer upon layer of distance between them—something he found ridiculously easy to identify second time around—but she turned her head to look at him and he saw unexpected warmth in her eyes. This couldn't be easy for her, listening to all of this, but she was generous enough to let herself feel compassion for the woman who had claimed his heart first. The two flickering Jennies who had been dizzying him all evening stood still for a second and, slowly, one started to fade.

'It wasn't long before her behaviour began to change,' he said. 'I found out she was missing her therapy sessions. Her new friends lived a really fast lifestyle, I later discovered. I didn't want to believe it at first, but it became obvious that she was using again.'

Jennie put her hands over her mouth. 'Oh, Alex! That's awful!'

He'd been devastated when he'd worked it all out. He'd known she was stronger than that. She didn't have to just…*give in*…and run away into a chemical world. They could have sorted things out together. But she hadn't trusted him to be strong for her.

Jennie pulled the throw tighter around her shoulders and tucked her hands away inside it. 'What did you do?'

He shrugged. 'I confronted her about it.'

'Did it do any good?'

He shook his head, partly to answer her question, partly because he still couldn't believe the way Becky had erupted that night. The simmering resentment that he'd been able to taste in the air each time he'd come home had ignited like petrol vapour.

'I suspected she was under the influence of something because she just went crazy, blaming me for everything—even the fact that she wasn't pregnant yet. Apparently, I was a useless husband, too interested in his career to be any use to a woman. She even said she'd do better to look elsewhere for a father for her children.'

Jennie's eyes widened. He knew the question behind her look: *had she?*

Not even fit enough to be a sperm donor, that was what Becky had said to him. A deep hole opened up inside him, but he sucked it closed again by sheer willpower.

'I don't know,' he said in reply to Jennie's silent question. 'At the time I thought she was just venting, but later I started to wonder if she'd already started her search.'

And recent events had confirmed his suspicions. He opened his mouth, ready to tell her everything, ready to reveal the vital detail he'd left out of the conversation until now, but hesitated. While Jennie had stopped looking daggers at him, he wasn't sure she was ready to hear it. Emotional women needed to be handled with kid gloves. He'd learned that the hard way with Becky. And Jennie could be unpredictable. He didn't want to scare her away again by revealing too much too soon. He needed to lay more groundwork, make sure she understood everything first.

Jennie shuffled forward in her chair. 'What made you think that?'

He exhaled sharply. 'We argued for hours, but eventually she promised she'd keep her therapy appointments, that we'd try to put what had been going wrong in our marriage right, but the next day, when I came home from work, she was gone. I don't think she'd have done that if she hadn't had somewhere to go to, some*one* to go to.'

'Gone?' Jennie sat up so straight so quickly that the throw slipped off her shoulders. She didn't seem to notice.

Alex rubbed his forehead with his thumb and forefinger. 'She'd taken her car, cleared out her wardrobe—and the savings account.'

Jennie just shook her head, mirroring the confusion he'd felt when he'd finally pieced it all together, then she got up and came to stand close to him. Not too close, though. 'Why did she do that? Take the money?'

Alex shrugged. He'd made himself crazy trying to work that one out. The only thing he'd come up with was that she must have been very, very angry. 'I think she wanted to punish me.'

All he'd ever wanted was to look after Becky. How had he got it so wrong?

He stopped pacing and looked bleakly at Jennie. He could tell she was chewing it all over. She looked sad for him, but he didn't deserve her compassion. He should have paid attention to what was going on sooner. Good husbands were supposed to notice whether their wives were happy or not. He paused for a moment, trying to assimilate the revelation that had sneaked into his mind while he'd been looking at Jennie. It seemed he hadn't learnt as much as he should have done from the whole Becky fiasco. He was making the same mistakes all over again.

When he'd proposed to Jennie, he'd really thought he'd never have to worry about her being emotionally vulnerable. She was warm and giving—tough, he'd thought. And she was sophisticated and charming, born to the world he now lived in, navigating it with ease. Why would there have been a problem? She was *nothing* like Becky.

That was why her departure from the hotel in Paris had been such a shock; he just hadn't seen it coming, had thought Jennie would cope marvelously, as she always did. Standing in the hotel lobby, he'd felt sick and empty. His new wife had done a disappearing act, just like the first one. For a man who was supposed to be a textbook definition of a runaway success, two runaway wives was not a good track record.

'Oh, Alex,' she said softly. 'Why couldn't you share any of this with me? I would have understood.'

He clamped his lips together and thought about her question. It hadn't seemed necessary to fill her in on the details of his past. It wasn't something he liked to talk about. It had taken him quite some time to glue himself back together, to feel normal again. Okay, maybe not normal, exactly, but stable. He'd eventually managed to squash all the deep, dark things he'd been feeling into a compartment at the back of his mind.

Sure, he'd had to lock a lot of other things away with them—hope, joy, peace—but he was feeling cynical about those things anyway, and the loss was bearable because he hadn't had to deal with those darker emotions.

So when the divorce papers had arrived at his home a year later he'd been ready for them. He'd clinically been able to accept that whatever his first wife had felt for him was dead…and he was the one who'd killed it.

For a long time after that he'd shied away from relationships, but then he'd met Jennie and she'd filled his life with sunshine. Childish of him, perhaps, not to have told her more, but he'd just wanted to leave that compartment shut, enjoy her warmth uninterrupted for a while, had just wanted to be happy.

He delved into his consciousness for the right answer. 'I was ashamed,' he finally admitted. 'I'm not proud of how I handled the situation with Becky, or happy that she made a complete and utter fool of me. And I thought it had nothing to do with *our* future together.'

Jennie started pacing now, all the while keeping her eyes on him. 'Well, since it almost blew our future to smithereens, I'd say you were a little short-sighted on that point.'

Touché.

'If I'd understood the situation,' she said, looking exasperated, 'if I'd known all about Becky, I might have been less—melodramatic—about the whole thing. A good relationship requires communication, Alex—not telepathy! If we don't start to talk to each other, this marriage will never survive.'

He looked at his hands. She was right. He'd been blind, made another bad call, when he'd been so convinced he'd been doing the right thing. He'd spent so long walking on eggshells around Becky, protecting her from anything that might upset her fragile balance, that he'd got used to keeping everything to himself. But Jennie wasn't like that, hadn't needed his babying. He thought about her words again and had a sudden second surge of hope.

'Are you saying *you* want this marriage to survive?'

She bit her lip, nibbling at a loose bit of skin. 'Maybe,' she replied, almost whispering.

When he'd arrived at the hotel this evening he wasn't sure he'd even wanted to hear that. He'd been too angry to think straight. But underneath that anger—and possibly fuelling it a little—had been an ache to see her again. To be with her. To know this had all been a horrible nightmare.

He walked over to her, touched her cheeks tenderly with both hands and then kissed her, briefly, with aching softness. Jennie closed her eyes and tears slid down her face again. She pulled away, looked at him in confusion.

'I don't know, Alex. I just don't know. You turning up again, all this information, in just a few hours… It's a lot to deal with. I'm exhausted…'

She was shaking under his fingers. He'd never seen her like this, so close to the edge of losing her ever-present sophisticated cool. He didn't want to be reminded of Becky at this point, but he had to allow for the fact that he might be pushing too hard, too fast, not considering Jennie's feelings.

'Why don't you get some sleep?' he said softly and nodded to the vast bedroom.

'What about you?' she said, hugging herself with both arms.

He gave her a wan smile. 'Brain's too busy. I'm going to stay out here. We can talk again in the morning.'

She nodded, and retreated into the bedroom. Before she shut the door, she turned. 'Goodnight, Alex,' she said, then closed it softly.

He sat on the sofa for a long time, trying to work out how to tell her everything else. He sighed. There was a shred of hope now that he might save this marriage, but only a tiny shred. One false move and he'd ruin everything again.

But what if they tried and it was all too much for her? What if she didn't cope the way he'd thought she would? He'd made these assumptions before and his whole life had collapsed. He couldn't ignore the fact that he could be setting both of them up for disaster.

Jennie woke for what seemed like the thousandth time in the last two weeks to find the bed too empty. She'd rebelled against that sensation at first, spreading herself out like a starfish as she went to sleep, filling as much of the space as she could, but she always woke to find herself curled up in a ball on her side of the bed, the flat cold space next to her a constant reminder. She hadn't even bothered to try last night.

This morning every muscle in her body was stiff and uncooperative. She did her best to stretch out the kinks as she lay there, then slid out of bed and walked over to the dressing table to look in the mirror.

Oh, help.

Despite the fact she'd been physically and emotionally exhausted last night, she'd struggled to get past that drowsy first stage of sleep. Memories and fears, mixed with other random images, had danced round and round inside her head, leaving her dizzy and disoriented. To be honest, she wasn't feeling much better now.

She blinked to try and clear the grit from her eyes, then scurried into the bathroom for a shower, an unwarranted sense of urgency chasing her. She emerged fresher, but hardly more relaxed. She hadn't noticed it before, but Marion must have had her overnight bag transferred from her old room some time the previous evening, because it was sitting on the suitcase rack beside the wardrobe. She dressed in neutral tones, comfy trousers and a soft jumper, and brushed her hair into a low, short ponytail.

Alex had seen her all dishevelled and bare of make-up many times. It was silly to be smearing the foundation on, covering the purple smudges under her eyes with concealer, but last night she'd been a mess in every way possible and she felt the need to recover lost ground this morning.

When she'd finished getting ready she pushed the bedroom door open gently and peered into the living room, every nerve on alert. The silent winter light gave the room a frosty appearance. At first she thought he'd gone, maybe to pay her back for doing the same to him, but then she heard a soft breath and noticed an arm draped over the edge of the sofa.

She took a few steps forward, her eyes never leaving his sleeping form. He was crunched into a most uncomfortable-looking position, the elegant sofa too short to accommodate his long legs. Jennie didn't know whether to be insulted that he hadn't even *tried* to climb into the super king-sized bed next door with her, or to be impressed by his chivalry.

One of his fingers twitched and she took a step back, held her breath.

Alex opened his eyes. Not with the soft fluttering some people did. They were suddenly wide open, fully alert. He had the most irritating habit of making the transition from fully asleep to fully awake in a split-second, while it normally took Jennie a good hour and a couple of cups of cappuccino to reach full consciousness.

He found her instantly, and as his gaze met hers she didn't doubt that she was fully in focus. Alex was a man who didn't perceive blurred edges. Everything was off or on, right or wrong, black or white.

He gathered his limbs together in one smooth motion and stood up, ran his hand through hair so short it couldn't possibly be messy.

'Good morning,' she said quietly. And then, because she was feeling too awkward to let the silence hang between them, she added, 'Did you sleep well?'

He looked at the sofa and then back at her. 'I slept at some point. That's enough.'

Jennie smiled nervously at him. What next? Where did they go from here?

She'd never been awkward around Alex, but it seemed so surreal, being in the same room as him after all this time. On some level they felt like strangers all over again. There was so much she didn't know about her husband, but what he'd told her last night had just been history—people and dates and events. Just facts and figures when you boiled it all down. But the first time she'd met Alex she'd felt as if she'd really understood him on some instinctive, elemental level, almost as if she'd *recognized* him, even though they'd never met before. Did finding out all of this... history...of his change that? She'd have guessed not, but this morning everything *felt* different, and now she wasn't sure.

She wanted to lick her lips, ask him casually where they were now, but her mouth had dried into a polite little smile.

So here they were in no-man's-land—open hostility put off for the moment, but still a long way from where they once had been.

Alex opened his mouth, took a breath, but before he could make a sound there was a discreet knock on the door.

'Come in,' he called, sounding infuriatingly unbothered by the interruption.

Marion poked her head round the door and smiled approvingly at the pair of them. 'Just wanted to let you know that we're all meeting for brunch at ten-thirty in the dining room.' She looked expectantly at them, smiling.

Jennie and Alex shared a look.

'That's very kind, Marion,' he said, not once

taking his eyes off Jennie, 'but I think a quiet breakfast is more what we had in mind.'

Her stepmother's smile upgraded itself into a beam. 'Marvellous. We'll see you both later, I expect.' And, without waiting for goodbyes, she clicked the door closed.

Alex ran his fingers through his hair again and exhaled, showing the first sign that he was more agitated than Jennie had supposed.

'Can you hang on for ten minutes?' he asked, his eyes darting towards the bedroom door. 'I could do with a shower.'

Jennie just nodded mutely, the sudden thought of Alex alone in the shower not helping her current difficulty with speech.

He pulled an overnight bag from behind the sofa. He must have had it in his car and collected it while she'd been sleeping. But that was Alex all over—prepared for every conceivable situation, while she, on the other hand, liked to fly by the seat of her lacy French knickers.

She kept clear of the bedroom while Alex showered, and he emerged a short while later looking all mouth-watering and distant, hardly glancing her way as he collected his watch off the sideboard and slipped on his shoes.

Jennie sneaked a look at her own watch. It was just before eight. Hopefully, the rest of the wedding party who'd stayed at the hotel would be far too hungover to stagger down to breakfast at this time of day. She and Alex should be able to talk in relative privacy. And talk they must. She might have been tired and over-emotional last night, but it hadn't taken long during her tossing and turning in bed to remember that Alex still hadn't told her everything.

Okay, she understood now why he'd needed to go to Becky and, while she still wasn't ready to be happy about it, she wasn't filled with fear about it any more. Even after a couple of weeks she'd been driving herself crazy trying to work out why Alex had gone, why he kept delaying his return to her. But to be in that state of limbo for *four years?* It would have driven her insane. If Becky had had things to say to him to ease her conscience and release Alex before she died, then he'd needed to hear them. It would probably be better for their fledgling marriage in the long run if Alex could put the past to rest, but...

That didn't explain why he'd *stayed* in London for almost a week.

Yesterday he'd hinted he had something big to

tell her, something that might make her want to ditch him altogether. Had he just been exaggerating and had told her this big 'thing' last night, or was the revelation still to come? She knew what she wanted to believe, but a sense of foreboding had settled over her like frost in the night and she couldn't shake it.

Until she knew, they couldn't even hope to start planning a future together. Everything hung on what Alex would say this morning—her life, her dreams, her dignity—and she wanted to get it over and done with. She'd waited long enough.

They made it halfway down to the restaurant before any hopes of a quiet tête-à-tête over coffee and croissants were dashed. As they turned at one of the large square landings on the staircase, they caught up with Auntie Barb, who was looking chirpier than she had a right to.

Jennie didn't have time to backtrack up the stairs, dragging Alex with her. She didn't even manage to outmanoeuvre an orange kiss. But the ordeal was over quickly because her aunt was much more interested in checking out the man she was with.

She batted her lashes at him. 'I don't think

we had the pleasure of meeting last night, Mr...
er...'

'Dangerfield,' Alex said without holding out
his hand, and looking vaguely impatient.

'Well, Mr Dangerfield, it's lovely to meet any
friend of Jennifer's.' She suddenly remembered
her niece's presence and turned to her, all syrup
and sweetness. 'So kind of you to offer your room
to poorly old me last night,' she said. Then she
leaned in close and added in a lower voice, 'It's
this arthritis of mine. It wears me out unexpectedly sometimes.'

Jennie bit back a cackle of laughter. 'No problem,' she said smoothly.

But Auntie Barb wasn't going to be shaken
off that easily. 'Why don't we all have breakfast together?' She paused to look at Alex, her
jovial smile gaining a slightly predatory edge.
'We didn't get a chance to chat last night and you
can catch me up on the latest scrape you've got
yourself into.'

Jennie just kept smiling.

He's standing right next to me, actually.

'That's a lovely idea, Auntie Barbara, but I've
just remembered I've left my...er...in my room.

I better just go and...' She jerked her thumb towards to the top of the staircase.

'Never mind,' her aunt replied, not looking crestfallen in the slightest. 'That'll give Mr Dangerfield and I a chance to get to know each other better while we wait for you.'

Jennie grabbed for Alex's hand and felt him start. She gripped harder. 'Oh, but Al—Mr Dangerfield—needs to come and help me look,' she said, nodding hard and willing him to play along.

Alex looked both solemn and irritated for a second, and then he bestowed one of his rare smiles on Auntie Barb. Jennie's heart thudded to a stop. He really should have warned her he was going to do that. When Alex smiled, the effect was devastating.

It wasn't just that it transformed his face, made him seem less intimidating, more approachable. No, the thing that took one's breath away was being the object of all that concentrated focus. The woman in question felt as if the smile was one hundred per cent hers, that he might never smile that way again at any other woman for the rest of his life...

'I can't leave a lady in distress, now, can I?' he said ruefully.

Auntie Barb just nodded understandingly.

'Maybe we'll bump into each other later,' he added.

And then Jennie and Alex were running back up the stairs, hand in hand, leaving Auntie Barb to mutter, 'Oh, I *do* hope so,' to herself in a wistful voice.

CHAPTER SIX

'WE HAVE to get out of here,' Jennie whispered at him when they'd reached the top of the stairs. She kept running, pulling him along behind her, until they were tucked away down a little side corridor. She stopped and rested against the wall, panting a little. Alex couldn't stop watching the rise and fall of her collarbone as she craned her neck towards the staircase to see if another random family member was about to appear.

All he could think about was leaning in close and tasting her there.

Jennie looked unusually serious. 'If we go downstairs,' she said, 'my whole family will accost us one by one. They'll want to know who you are, why they didn't see you last night and why you're here now.'

His previously optimistic mood plummeted. Last night he'd thought he'd been wrong about her, had judged her too harshly, but now he wasn't sure.

She was staring at him, waiting for him to say something. When he didn't answer, her perfectly plucked brows wrinkled slightly. 'What?' she said, shaking a single wisp of hair that had escaped her ponytail out of her eyes.

'Still trying to hide your dirty little secret?' he said.

She rubbed her forehead with her fingertips, but the frown increased. 'What dirty little secret?'

'Me,' he said simply.

She shook her head. 'It's not like that!'

He glanced at the stairs, waited until she followed his gaze. 'Then why don't we go downstairs, hand in hand, and you can introduce me to your family properly? No more sneaking around, Jennie. I'm tired of it.'

She opened her mouth and shut it again. 'But I…I can't.'

The whole situation had him on edge. He was finding it impossible to stand outside of himself, be objective—something he made a very good living out of. His thoughts became dark and sarcastic. Of course she didn't want to tell her family. Getting carried away and eloping had been glamorous and exciting but, when it came down to it, neither of them were sure she was in it for the long haul—he'd seen the uncertainty in her eyes this morning. It had haunted him all the while he'd been in the shower.

But there were too many things haunting him at present, so he banished the feeling with a little biting humour. 'Of course you can. Think of the stir it'll create. You'll be chief topic of conversation for weeks, maybe even months. What's not to like? Unless, of course…' he leaned in close—too close '…you're ashamed of me.'

She slid along the wall a little to escape him, her full lips pouting slightly. 'That's not fair, Alex.'

Probably not. But he was on a roll, and it felt good to finally say all the things that had been circuiting his head for a couple of weeks.

'Isn't it? Then what other reason can you give me for getting married, not telling a soul—not even your parents—and then running away and pretending it never happened? Daddy's not going to clear the mess up for you this time, sweetheart. I'm one problem you're going to have to solve yourself.'

She glared at him. 'You're being deliberately nasty, twisting things…'

He shrugged. 'Then convince me otherwise.'

Jennie's bottom slid a couple of inches down the wall and her shoulders wilted. 'Alex, how do we explain...*us*...to my family? Seriously? Even we don't know where we stand with each other at the moment!'

She had a point there. But that was the problem with Jennie Hunter—normally rational, sensible men got all riled up when she was around and let their emotions have a part in the decision-making process. It wasn't the way he usually did things. Perhaps a bit of fresh air and distance from this pressure cooker situation would help.

'Okay. Let's go somewhere else.' Constant ducking away from nosy relatives would just keep their adrenalin spiking and they both needed to be calm if they were going to discuss their future.

'But where?' Jennie said. 'It's half eight on a Sunday morning. Nothing's open for hours yet.'

'We're just over the border from Kent, and Elmhurst is less than an hour away,' he said, mentally pulling up a map of the county and marking out the best route home.

Jennie looked uncomfortable, and he didn't begrudge her that. If things had turned out differently, they'd have both been living in the spacious farmhouse on the outskirts of the village now. He'd imagined them coming home from their honeymoon, weary and happy, laughing at their own silliness as he carried her over the threshold.

'We'd have all the time and privacy we need,' he added. The house was going to be empty until early evening. Plenty of time to break the news to Jennie.

She bit her top lip and then let it slide past her teeth slowly. 'Okay,' she finally said.

He nodded, looking more confident and sure of a satisfactory outcome than he felt. He hoped to high heaven that she didn't set one foot inside the door and decide to run again.

The winter sky was a pure cool grey, lit from below by a sun that refused to stray far from the horizon. The previous night had been clear, full of stars, and now a crunchy frost covered the fields and hedgerows. Jennie sat in silence as Alex drove them down virtually empty country roads to the small Kent village of Elmhurst.

She'd been to Alex's house many times before, had always loved the rolling countryside, dotted with farmhouses, and little hamlets with steepled churches, but this visit was different. It wasn't a game any more. They weren't in the throes of a whirlwind romance, sneaking off to spend time with each other whenever they could. Just going inside the front door would remind her of all that should have been, but wasn't.

Her bathrobe should have been hanging on the back of Alex's bathroom door. Her toothbrush should have been nestling up to his in the pot by the washbasin. Her clothes should have been filling half—okay, probably a lot more than half— of Alex's wardrobe. But it was a month after her wedding day and she wasn't really occupying any space in his life at all.

She closed her eyes and tried to relax the muscles in her neck. Had it only been hours ago that her and Alex's lives had collided again? She'd felt and thought so many conflicting things during that time that it seemed a lot longer, and now she seemed cast adrift on a lake of confusion.

On one hand, the man she'd pledged her life to had sought her out, just as she'd wanted him to, but on the other hand, there were multiple reasons not to trust the inward tugging that was slowly drawing her back into his orbit. Yes, she knew now that he'd done what he'd done because it had been part of his strict moral code, that he'd been acting nobly, but what if things like this cropped up in the future? Obviously, there wouldn't be another dying first wife, but there would be other things he felt compelled to do.

She wasn't sure she wanted to be in a marriage where she played second fiddle to her husband's lofty ideals. She supposed she could cultivate some lofty ideals of her own, but that kind of thing didn't come naturally to her. What if her critics were right, and she didn't have it in her to be that mature and unselfish?

No, if they decided to patch things up and go forward, they were going to have to promise each other that the relationship came first, and that nothing and nobody should be allowed to get in the way of that. It was what she'd thought they'd done already, after all. Wasn't that what marriage was all about?

They made good time, and it wasn't more than forty minutes before they pulled into the driveway of his small manor house. Unlike the local stately home, Elmhurst Hall, Alex's home was only just verging on grand, the home of a gentleman farmer in years gone by. It was a large square, two-storey building with tall multi-paned

sash windows and red brickwork that had weath-
ered into a dull rust colour.

She'd expected the windows to be dark when
they pulled up, but there was a faint orange glow
from the ground floor windows on the left side of
the house where the kitchen was, and there was
a car she didn't recognize parked in the drive.
Alex brought the car to a halt and put the hand-
brake on, but when she moved to open the door
he placed a hand on her arm. She let go of the
door handle and looked at him.

'Before we go in…'

Jennie's heart started to pump. The way he was
looking at her was making her very nervous. She
saw doubt in his eyes, hesitation. And Alex never
hesitated about anything. Once he'd made his
mind up to do something, that was it.

'What is it?' she said quietly.

He looked ahead out of the windscreen at the
house, in the direction of the orange glow. 'I
thought they'd planned to be out this morning, but
there must have been a hiccup in the timetable…
I have someone staying with me—a relative.'

'Oh.' She frowned again. She seemed to be
doing a lot of that at present. Now she was just
confused. Alex had said they'd have space and

privacy, and now they were going to have to tiptoe around a house guest? The whole point of leaving the hotel had been to avoid bothersome relatives. But, before she could think of anything to ask him about the situation, he was out of the driver's door and striding round the car to open hers.

Jennie just blinked. Her husband might be an enigma, but one couldn't fault his manners.

She eased herself from the car seat elegantly and nodded her thanks, then followed him up to the front door. The inside of the house was different, too. It smelled different. Before, it hadn't really had an aroma. If she'd had to describe it, she'd have said Alex's house smelled clean, and faintly of leather. Now, however, there were warm baking smells drifting from the kitchen—cinnamon and butter and toffee. There were extra coats on the hooks by the front door and the sound of a radio tuned to a pop station somewhere in the distance.

'I'll introduce you quickly, and then we can talk,' he said seriously.

Jennie nodded, knowing that the quicker she did what Alex asked, the sooner they'd reach a decision about their future, one way or the other.

She was sick of waiting, sick of something else always butting in and getting in the way. At last she was going to have her husband's full attention, and she was going to make it count.

He led her into the kitchen and the first person Jennie saw was a woman, maybe a little bit younger than she was, bending to remove some delicious-smelling muffins from the oven. The woman had wavy dark hair cut into a bob and her eyes were warm and smiling when she turned to greet Alex. There was a flicker of hesitation as she saw Jennie standing there, but her smile didn't falter.

'Perfect timing,' she said, her gaze transferring back to Alex and warming even further. Jennie realised she was doing that thing her father said she did with her lip again and smiled back at the woman to iron it out.

'This is Toni—my cousin,' Alex said.

'Nice to meet you,' Toni said, nodding at Jennie, but displaying hands floury enough to preclude any other form of greeting. 'The kettle boiled not long ago. Do you both want coffee?'

'Hi,' Jennie said. 'And yes, please.'

It seemed bizarre, smiling and making

small talk while her whole future hung in the balance.

'And this is Mollie,' Alex added, and Jennie suddenly noticed a little girl—of about two or three, she guessed, not being very good at that type of thing—sitting at the kitchen table. She had dark hair caught into two low bunches, and the ends were threatening to dangle themselves into the gloopy muffin mix she was stirring with great care. At the mention of her name, the little girl looked up at them and blinked.

'Hello, Mollie.'

Alex swallowed. 'Girls…this is…um… Jennie.'

'Hello,' Mollie said, and then returned to what she was doing. Toni just smiled again, wiped her hands, then opened one of the kitchen cupboards and took out a cafetière.

It hadn't escaped Jennie's attention that Alex had been economical with the introductions, mentioning names but leaving their marital relationship out of the equation, and it gave her an unexpected boost. She wasn't the only one to chicken out of coming clean to the family, then. And the knowledge helped her feel less wrong-footed by the whole situation. For all Alex's high-handedness about her reluctance to spill the beans to her relatives, he'd done exactly the same thing, meaning he was just as wary about the future as she was.

Despite Alex's impatient fidgeting, Toni was making the coffee at a leisurely pace and Jennie decided to distract herself from the strange undercurrents circling beneath this charming scene of domesticity by taking an interest in Mollie's cookery while Toni told Alex something about not being able to have Sunday lunch at her house because one of her boys had chickenpox and she didn't want Mollie to get it.

'What are you making?' Jennie said, and sat down in the empty chair next to the little girl.

Mollie didn't answer for a second, too intent on mashing a lump out of the cake mix.

'Muffins,' she said without looking up at Jennie. She carried on mixing until Toni retrieved the bowl and motioned for Mollie to put crinkly paper cases into a deep-holed baking tin.

Well, every family had its quirks, and it looked as if she was going to have to get used to Alex's side's silence and cryptic looks. But surely little girls weren't supposed to follow that pattern? Weren't they supposed to chatter on to anybody, given the chance? She certainly had. Her nanny had always complained they couldn't leave the house without Jennie giving at least five people her life story and treating them to an impromptu dance recital.

But what did she know, anyway? She didn't run into many children in her line of work. Most of her parties involved cocktails and expensive goodie bags, not jelly and ice cream.

Toni declared the coffee ready and Jennie turned to find Alex staring at her, a new and unreadable expression in his eyes.

She raised her eyebrows. *What?*

Just like the little girl beside her had done, he took his time answering, all the while watching her intently, and then something changed—*clicked*—as if he'd made a decision of some kind.

'Shall we?' he said as he took the tray Toni offered him and motioned towards the kitchen door with it.

'Of course.' She looked over her shoulder as they left the room. 'Thanks for the coffee,' she said.

Toni just nodded.

And then Jennie was following Alex down the

wide hallway, full of black and white prints, and into his study. He placed the tray on his spotless glass desk. She didn't wait to be asked, just sat herself in one of the comfy armchairs that framed the fireplace and waited while Alex poured the coffee and handed her a cup.

He sat opposite her in an identical chair and sipped his coffee, watching her, wearing that same expression he'd had in the kitchen. Eventually, she couldn't stand the silence any longer. She put her cup down on a side table and knotted her fingers before resting her hands on her knees.

'So…Alex.'

He looked totally impassive, calm. Just the tiniest flicker of his eyelashes at her words betrayed him.

There'd been too much heavy silence on the car journey and she couldn't bear more of it now, so she took a breath and dived in. 'What do you want, Alex? From me? For us? Where do we go from here?'

He leaned down and placed his coffee cup on the cold hearth. 'I know I hurt you,' he said, and paused for a while. She could see him processing it all, could almost hear the words inside his head. 'I didn't mean to. I assumed too much.'

She nodded. Hadn't she done the same? She'd assumed Alex's leaving was the same kind of leaving she'd had to deal with all her life. The kind of leaving where people disappeared and you had to *make* them want to come back, and even then it was no good sometimes. Sometimes they just left a hole that was never filled, no matter how much sparkly stuff you disguised it with.

She looked him in the eye. There'd been so much she'd wanted to say to him, so much she'd wanted to spit and yell at him, but suddenly she understood the beauty of his silence. As they sat staring at each other, she knew they both understood they'd acted short-sightedly. Maybe because they'd both assumed they'd known each other when they hadn't.

Did that mean they could start building a future again, or did it mean they were so incompatible they never would?

The fear of being second place had kept her from knowing that Alex had spoken the truth when he'd left her in Paris. She didn't know what or why, but it was suddenly clear to her that he wouldn't have left her alone if there'd been any other way, and he would have come for her. *Had* come for her. Not on her timescale, obviously, but that wasn't the way that Alex worked. He was a man who kept his promises, but she didn't have much experience with that kind of man, only with men who intended to keep their promises but somehow something more important came up in the meantime.

Her father had always promised they'd go to the park *next* weekend. But there'd always been a meeting, a round of golf with an important contact, a trip to Belgium, or Frankfurt or Rome. So, to Jennie, promises weren't something she could hold in her hands, knowing they were solid... real. Promises were misty things. Left to their own devices, they didn't deliver the goods. She had to chase them, catch them, pin them down until they became concrete.

And thoughts of his promise to return to her led to thoughts of other promises—ones they'd exchanged and marked with rings. She hadn't thought to check, but she looked now and saw the gold band she'd placed on his finger still there. Her heart did an Olympic standard triple flip.

He'd kept his ring on.

She hadn't noticed it last night, but that didn't mean it hadn't been there. Or had he replaced it this morning? She really wasn't sure. Almost instinctively, she reached for the charm bracelet on her right wrist, felt for the matching band hanging from it, disguised by all the other glittering things catching the light and flashing it around.

Everything that had been fogged with confusion for the last few weeks suddenly became clear. Frighteningly so.

Alex would never let go of any promise lightly; he'd cling on doggedly, sometimes to the point of stupidity. Loyalty was important to him. So now she had to ask herself whether or not she wanted his loyalty, whether she *wanted* him to keep the promises he'd made to her.

'You haven't answered my question,' she said, drowning out the one ringing in her head.

Let him say the right things, she silently pleaded. Let him make it easier for me. I can't jump into this abyss again if he's not with me. It would be too cold, and far too lonely.

But Alex didn't say anything. He walked towards her until he was within touching distance. Jennie felt herself start to shake, little quivers beginning in her knees that vibrated up her spine. He was giving her that deep, hooded look that had always done this to her, even though, most of the time, she didn't have a clue what was going on inside his head.

And then he reached forward and touched her face. His fingertips were so soft, so gentle, as they explored her cheekbone. It had always astounded her that a man who seemed to have himself so tightly leashed could be quite so tender, that he could express just a little of what he felt without it bursting out of him like water destroying a dam.

Her eyelids closed. Surely she should flinch from his touch? Surely she shouldn't sway towards him, the breath held in her lungs? She felt him come closer. The fingers of his other hand slid through her hair to the back of her neck and he gently pulled her closer. She didn't even try to resist. Just placed her palms on his chest. Not because she wanted to shove him away, but just because she suddenly couldn't last another moment without touching him.

The kiss started off as slow and soft as his first touch, but it wasn't tentative or testing. Alex wanted this as much as she did. Probably more so, because his actions were always so sure and confident, based on iron-clad decisions that had been made after extensive research and pondering.

She, however, hadn't really even made a conscious decision to fall back into Alex's arms and into his life. Right now, in this moment, it just felt right.

The kiss didn't stay soft and graceful for long. They still had it—that intoxicating chemistry that had knocked them both sideways the first time they'd met—and Alex's hands were soon around her waist, clamping her to him. She wrapped her arms around his neck, meeting him, urging him.

And then he lifted her and for a second she was suspended in his arms, before her bottom met the slightly cool, smooth glass of his desk. She hooked a calf around the back of his knees, keeping him pressed up against her, and her fingers searched for the top button of his shirt.

Alex made a sound that was part laugh, part moan and dipped his head lower to kiss her neck. Jennie gave up with the shirt buttons after just two or three, frustrated by her own clumsiness. It was too slow. She needed to feel his warm skin under her fingertips. Nothing else mattered.

She grabbed a handful of his shirt and yanked it out from the back of his jeans, but froze when the door handle creaked.

Suddenly Alex was two feet away, doing up his buttons with as much success as she'd had in undoing them, and Jennie was sliding off the desk. Her feet had just hit the carpet when the door opened. She ran a hand through her hair, half pulled out of her ponytail, as Mollie's dark head appeared.

'Muffins ready,' she announced solemnly, not even blinking at Alex's unusually untidy appearance.

Alex flashed a look at Jennie, who felt herself blush. While it was perfectly okay—expected, even—for newly-weds to behave in the manner they'd been, she'd forgotten entirely that they weren't alone in the house, that maybe there was a better place, or time, for what they'd been about to get up to.

'I'm just…um…talking with Jennie,' he said.

The tips of Jennie's ears burned. As far as she remembered, they'd only managed a couple of sentences each before things had gone astray.

'I'll…we'll…be along to the kitchen in just a minute to have one,' he added.

Just before the door closed properly, Jennie heard her soft little voice one more time. Mollie fixed Alex with her clear, pale eyes. 'Okay, Daddy.'

Jennie felt cold air rush past her cheeks and into the very roots of her hair as he shook his head and Mollie shut the door.

Daddy?

Had Mollie just called Alex *Daddy?*

CHAPTER SEVEN

FOR the first time in their relationship, Alex was aware that the tables had been well and truly turned. He was the one dropping the bombshell, doing something totally crazy and unexpected, and Jennie was the innocent bystander, the one trying to make sense of it all. He'd thought being on the other side of the equation would have given him a sense of power, but it only left him with a lead weight in his stomach, one that was growing heavier with every blink of her incredulous eyes.

Things had been going so well. Too well, maybe.

He'd been on the verge of telling her before Mollie had opened the door. He'd brought Jennie to his study so he could sit her down and methodically fill in the holes of the explanation he'd given her last night. But all those careful explanations had gone out of the window when Jennie had sat in that leather armchair and looked at him with the same hope and expectancy as she had on their wedding day. He hadn't been able to stop himself from walking over to her. Just one touch, he'd promised himself, and then he'd let the words out of his mouth.

He should have remembered how upside down and inside out she turned him, how she made every hair on his head stand on end and the adrenalin pump through his veins. He should have just stuck to one thing at a time.

Explaining first, touching later.

It wasn't as if he was good at explanations, anyway. Words just weren't his thing. Not that he felt clumsy with them, but they were just… unnecessary. He was better at showing how he felt by the things he did, by simply being the man he was. He sighed and ran a hand over the top of his head.

The shock in Jennie's eyes was quickly turning into something else. This was one time when he definitely should have stuck to the plan.

'You have a…? She's your…?'

He nodded again, reached for her. She couldn't back away, right up against the desk as she was, but she sidestepped him so fast she knocked the cafetière that had been sitting on the other side of the desk over and scalding coffee flowed all over the desk and dripped onto the floor.

She started to try and pick the cafetière up, but the hot liquid made her wince. It didn't stop her trying, though. She just kept attempting to right the glass jug, all the while looking panicked as more and more coffee sluiced around the table and made a thin, dark brown waterfall over the edge of the desk.

He reached across and held her hands, stopping her from burning herself, held them still and looked at her, until she understood that desks and carpets didn't matter. She looked back at him, blinking only once, and he couldn't decide whether she was going to cry or was getting ready to hit him over the head with the half-empty cafetière.

The silence was measured by the squelching *drip, drip, drip* of coffee hitting the carpet.

She pulled her hands away, stepped back. 'You have a daughter, and you never thought to tell me?'

'Until about three weeks ago, I didn't know… and I'm still not one hundred per cent sure.'

'How can you not know? What do you mean?'

He sighed. Where Becky had been concerned, he'd come to realise that just about anything was possible.

'Let me explain.'

This was the moment he'd been dreading. The moment when it all might get too much for his runaway bride. He could see the fear and uncertainty in her eyes. She looked for a long couple of seconds at the door.

'Please?' he added, and he couldn't ignore the vague hint of desperation in his voice. Neither could Jennie, it seemed. She stopped flashing angry looks at him and went and stood by the cold fireplace, her arms crossed.

Alex made his way back from the hospital cafeteria on autopilot. In the last day or so he'd done the journey so many times he didn't need to look at the signs to navigate the endless anonymous corridors back to the Intensive Care Unit.

As he entered the ward, he instantly went on red alert. Someone was talking loudly and emphatically and after the relentless serenity, punctured only by the drab electronic music of the machines that beeped and pinged and hissed in and out of time with each other, the noise seemed to reverberate off the walls.

Just before he turned into the section of corridor that led to Becky's room, a stout woman with a severe ponytail pushed past him, muttering something about not being a flipping free child-minding service. He quickened his pace and half-jogged to Becky's room, where he found the plump nurse who'd been there the other day when he'd arrived, holding a squirming toddler and wearing a dazed expression.

He'd seen so many nurses in the last thirty or so sleepless hours that he was almost surprised he recognised this one. But she'd stuck in his mind because, not long after he'd walked into this nightmare, she'd come quietly alongside him and asked if he was Alex. He'd nodded numbly, all the while looking at the broken body he hardly recognised amidst all the tubes and machines, and hadn't thought to wonder until later how she'd known.

The plump nurse, whose name he now noticed was Flora, had calmly told him that one of the paramedics who'd brought Becky in had said she'd whispered something before she'd lapsed into unconsciousness. He'd dutifully informed the staff in the Emergency Department, who'd passed it on to Flora or one of her colleagues. But Becky's last words must have suffered the 'Chinese whispers' effect because it hadn't made much sense.

Becky had grabbed the paramedic's hand and told him to tell Alex she belonged to him.

If the situation hadn't have been so dire, he might have allowed himself a dark chuckle at that. Becky hadn't been his in a long while. Hadn't wanted to be.

But he'd mulled the message over while he'd sat by her bedside, watching the ventilator puff air into her and then suck it out again, and he'd taken it to mean she wanted him to look after her, to be on her side. And since he was still listed on her donor card as her next of kin, the hospital had been happy to let him do that.

He supposed he should have been angry at her impudence, but he hadn't been able to feel anything but compassion for her in this state. And guilt, of course. He always felt the guilt. Becky had finally trusted him to look out for her, something he'd failed to do properly during their seven-year marriage. It helped mend something inside him that she'd at least given him this. He was going to make sure he did it properly this time, especially as things weren't looking promising. It was the least he could do for her.

Thank goodness Jennie understood. Well, just about understood. Even so, he wasn't looking forward to phoning her and telling her, once again, that he wouldn't be taking the two-hour train ride to Paris that evening.

He turned to Flora, who was doing her best to calm the grizzling child, and frowned.

'That woman? She just left her child here?'

Flora lost the battle and, rather than drop the child, she managed to set her down without too much of a bump. Both he and Flora watched as the little girl ran to the bed and stared at Becky.

'She says she's not hers,' Flora mumbled. 'Said she was just babysitting…'

Alex frowned. 'So whose is she, then?'

Flora didn't move and her gaze never left the bed. The little girl was pulling at Becky's hand, whimpering. 'Wake up,' she said in a tiny, thin voice.

A rock hit the bottom of Alex's stomach.

'Wake up, Mummy,' the girl wailed, then attempted to climb onto the bed beside her. But the bed was too high and her legs were too short, so she just held on to the pale hand nearest her. Her eyes filled with tears.

Becky had a child? A daughter?

He didn't know whether he ought to be happy or sad for her. Becky had got what she'd wanted—and quickly, too, he guessed. The girl had to be… what? Two?

'Is the man who was driving the car when Becky was injured her boyfriend?' he asked Flora.

She shrugged. 'I believe so. They moved him into one of the other wards earlier this afternoon.'

Alex looked down the hall but, before he could ask Flora where he could find the idiot who'd been driving too fast in the wrong direction down a one-way street, she laid a hand on his arm.

'It might be better if I go. If you wouldn't mind keeping an eye on her…' She nodded to the child. 'You know what to do if you need help.'

He nodded. Becky's alarms had gone off with worrying regularity since he'd been camped out here. He knew the drill and the nurses' station was a two-second sprint away.

While Flora was gone, he walked over to the little girl and crouched down. He tried talking to her, but she didn't acknowledge him. Not really. She kept staring at her mother, but blinked hard every time he started a new sentence. After a while, he gave up trying to talk and pulled a chair close so he could sit near her. He understood the need to be left alone with your own thoughts when you felt like this.

They stayed like that for quite a while and well before Alex heard Flora's footsteps in the hall outside he'd decided that making sure this little one was reunited with her family would be part of his debt to Becky. If he didn't, she'd be in foster care, just like her mother had been. Or, even worse, handed over to Becky's parents, and he'd breathe his last breath before he let that pack of hyenas mess this child up the way they had their daughter.

He breathed out. It felt good having a purpose, something concrete to do rather than sit here and wonder whether there'd be a miracle and Becky would open her eyes.

Eventually, the little girl turned and looked at him. He smiled. She didn't smile back, just yawned. He patted his lap.

'Would you like to come and sit here? You look tired.'

Slowly, she slid her hand out of Becky's and sidled over to him. She didn't reach out with confidence, as his cousin Toni's boys had done at that age, knowing he'd swing them into his arms. Instead, she backed up until her behind was touching his knee and lifted one leg in a tentative attempt to hoist herself up. He gently slid a hand under each armpit and eased her into his lap. Even though she yawned again, she didn't rest herself against him.

'What's your name?' he whispered.

She turned her head to look at him. 'Mollie,' she said quietly.

Alex looked into her big blue eyes and smiled. He should have known. Becky had always loved that name. When they'd been trying for a child of their own, she'd settled on it straight away.

And then something odd happened. It must be the lack of sleep, he'd thought at first, because he had the oddest sense of recognition as he and Mollie regarded each other. It was like looking at a photograph he knew by heart, which was strange because he'd never seen any photos of Becky as a child, so it couldn't be the resemblance to her mother that had registered something in his head. Anyway, Becky's eyes were hazel, not this clear, warm blue with a darker ring around the irises...

Like his.

And then the words that had been circuiting his head for the last couple of days unscrambled themselves and Alex felt himself plummet down a lift shaft that had opened up in the floor of the ICU.

Suddenly, Becky's last gasped message made sense.

Tell Alex she's his.

As Alex talked, Jennie folded her arms tighter across her middle, listening with growing horror. Horror at what Alex's shattered family had endured, and horror at her own adolescent foot-stamping when she hadn't got her own way.

Worse still, a little voice inside her head was prodding her to stamp some more, to put her hands on her hips and say it wasn't fair. To demand to know why Alex hadn't communicated any of this to her earlier. Had he done so, she might not have done such a thorough disappearing act.

But that was also a childish urge. She couldn't turn things around and blame Alex for her bad behaviour. He'd had a terrible situation to deal with—no wonder he'd sounded so spaced out when he'd managed to find time to call her—and he'd thought he'd married a grown-up, a woman who'd only days before had promised to stick with him through thick and thin. He'd had every right to ask for her understanding, and she'd had no right to deny it.

She sat down on the chair facing him and covered her face with her hands. 'I'm sorry, Alex. So sorry…'

'It wasn't your fault my first marriage was a runaway train,' he replied bleakly.

'No… I meant for the way I acted.' She moved one finger so she could peek at him from behind her hands and found him looking at her. She slid her hands apart and left them on her cheeks. He looked so weary, hardly any hint of the usual vital *Alex* energy she loved so much.

At least he wasn't angry with her any more. She could tell that from his eyes—they were no longer hard and icy. But he must be terribly disappointed in her. She should have been there for him. She should have been his shoulder to lean on. A wave of regret washed over her and she ached deep down to her toes. That time could never be bought back. She couldn't charm her way into having another shot, but she wished she could. She really wished she could.

'You said you weren't sure,' she muttered, as her brain continued to sort through the deluge of facts and images that had bombarded her at the beginning of this conversation. 'What did you mean by that?'

Alex peeled his gaze from hers and stared into the shadows of the fireplace. 'Just that. I'm still not sure that Mollie is my child.'

'But you said…'

Only his eyes moved as he glanced back in her direction. 'I know what Becky told the paramedic, but I have no idea if it's the truth.'

Jennie's hands slipped down her cheeks to cover her mouth. 'Do you really think…?'

Alex got up and went to stare out of the large bay window behind his desk. 'The woman—the babysitter—came back the next day to see Becky and apologise. It was too late by then, of course…'

Jennie stood up, wanting to go to him, but a sudden instinct told her to wait, to let him speak.

'Tracey was Becky's next door neighbour.' He

paused to make a disbelieving sound that might have been a laugh. 'I didn't even know Becky had moved back to London. The last I'd heard, she'd been in Southend.'

She took a step towards him. 'What did she tell you…this Tracey?'

'That the idiot driver had only been in Becky's life a few months, and that when Becky had first moved in next door she'd been living with another man—one she'd referred to as Mollie's daddy.' He shook his head. 'He's been out of the picture for a year or so now.'

'And you think…'

He looked over his shoulder at Jennie. 'It's possible,' he replied, then turned to the window again. She walked over and stood next to him, stared at the same fields and bare trees, watched the same rooks circling in the sky.

'Tomorrow morning everything will start opening up again after the Christmas break,' he said. 'I've got contacts who know how to get information—records—quickly. We'll see what the birth certificate says first.'

'And if it…' She couldn't quite bring herself to voice her doubts.

His shoulders slumped a little. 'Then there's DNA testing, just to make sure.'

Jennie was just about to place a palm on his shoulder blade when there was a knock at the door.

'Just a minute, Mollie. This is important.'

Jennie watched him, all of a sudden feeling as if Alex had just stepped out of a cocoon, transformed into something else. This was a father talking to his child. Alex was a father. She knew without a shadow of a doubt that the knowledge had changed him and there would be no going back. The Alex she'd shared a whirlwind romance with was gone. Instead of placing her hand on his shoulder, she smoothed down her jumper, then let her hands fall by her sides.

The door creaked open and Toni poked her head round the door.

'That was my other half on the phone,' she said, looking first at Alex and then at Jennie. 'He says another of the boys has started sprouting spots and that Jacob's spiking a fever.' She grimaced. 'I know I said I'd help out a bit longer, but I've got to go…'

Alex was already halfway across the room. 'Of

course you have,' he said as he put a hand on her arm. 'They're your children...'

Toni managed a little wave and Jennie reciprocated, but by the time she'd got her fingers aloft and wiggling, both Alex and his cousin had vanished down the hallway, talking in low tones.

It was only then she remembered the coffee, still dripping from the desk onto the floor, and she hurried to the kitchen to get a cloth. She could see Alex saying goodbye to Toni as she got in her car. Mollie was nowhere to be seen, but Jennie didn't think much of it as she ran a cloth under the tap and grabbed an armful of cleaning-type stuff from under the sink. Surely one of these sprays and potions was good for carpets?

She hadn't even got as far as reading the labels when Alex came striding back into the room. 'Where's Mollie?'

Jennie just looked at him. 'I don't know. I thought she was with you.'

A look of sheer panic crossed Alex's features, but before he could go into full crisis overdrive there was an ominous flushing sound from the downstairs bathroom. Did toddlers do that themselves these days? She really didn't know. She and Alex looked at each other, then dashed out of the study.

The scene in the downstairs bathroom wasn't pretty. Mollie was crying. There was a wet patch on the floor and a nappy wedged down the toilet. It was obvious that they hadn't heard the first flush, because it was jammed right down the bottom and the toilet bowl was almost full to the brim.

'No!' Alex yelled as Mollie reached for the handle to flush once more. She froze for a split second, then she closed her eyes, opened her mouth and the most terrifying sound emanated from it. It had the fluctuating pitch of a World War Two air raid siren, but was twice as loud.

Alex was obviously mortified to have caused that sound and looked helplessly at Jennie, his eyes begging. She looked at the devastation around her. Where did you start in situations like this? The floor? The loo? The air-raid siren? Alex was looking at her as if she was supposed to know. If her eardrums hadn't been vibrating past the point of comfort, she might have called him on that. As it was, she decided to let him deal with the blockage while she went to the source of her current pain. She took Mollie by the hand and led her back into the kitchen.

Once there, she knelt down beside her and rubbed her hand. 'It's okay, sweetheart. Don't cry.'

But Mollie's face was bright red and scrunched up into the most unappealing shape. And the noise just seemed to be getting louder.

She took Mollie's other hand and tried to make eye contact. 'Mollie. Mollie? Mollie…'

There was a brief hiccupping pause in the wailing and Jennie grabbed her chance. 'Did you have an accident, darling? Is that what the matter is?'

It was then that Jennie noticed the smell. Uh-oh. When she'd said the word *accident,* she hadn't really comprehended the full horror of the situation. A quick peek under Mollie's dress revealed the truth.

Jennie closed her eyes, gritted her teeth and picked the little girl up, trying not to think about how close her hands were to the source of the smell and whether it could seep through fabric. 'It's a bath for you, I think,' she said brightly, and bounced down the corridor and up the stairs.

She was obviously doing something wrong

because Mollie's face stopped scrunching and she looked at Jennie in surprise. The plus side? She'd shocked the siren into silence. Jennie decided she liked being looked at like an alien better than she did putting her ears through that noise, so she just kept bouncing.

To her complete relief, she found a stack of nappies and a pouch of those baby wipe things in the bathroom. She popped Mollie down on the floor, eased her dress over her head and threw it into the far corner of the bathroom. Then she peeled the girl's vest off and took off her sodden socks, using her thumb and forefinger like pincers. She'd just about finished when Alex appeared at the bathroom door, looking bemused and dishevelled.

'What now?' he said, looking hopefully at Jennie.

She gave him a wake-up-and-smell-the-coffee kind of look. Like she was supposed to know! Possession of an X chromosome did not give her access to some secret wisdom that could be called upon in toddler-related emergencies. Fashion-related emergencies, yes. But definitely not the kind that involved the stuff that was currently sliding down Mollie's left leg. *Euw.*

'Okay,' Alex said slowly, clearly getting the point. He looked at the shower cubicle. 'How about we stand her in there and just, well…hose her down?'

Jennie blinked. As good a plan as any. So they did just that. One problem. As soon as they turned the shower on, the siren started up again. Alex lunged towards the bath and turned on the taps.

Forty minutes later, Mollie was asleep on Alex's bed and Jennie and Alex were standing facing each other in his en suite bathroom.

'I think we wore her out,' Alex said with a smile.

Jennie couldn't help but chuckle. 'I think the feeling's mutual.'

For a brief second all the drama of the last few weeks faded away. Jennie almost didn't want to blink. This was more like the Alex she remembered: funny, in an understated way. Relaxed. Gorgeous. She sighed, and just that tiny noise was enough to pop the moment. The distinctive smell from Mollie's discarded dress made sure it stayed that way.

'Did you get the nappy out of the toilet?' she asked.

Alex made a face. 'Eventually.'

'What do you think she was trying to do?' Jennie asked as she folded a towel, then did it again, realising it was all lumpy and uneven.

Alex huffed out a breath and leant back against the tiled wall. 'Well, Toni tells me she thinks Mollie is just about potty trained.'

Jennie's eyebrows shot up. 'You think?'

There was that smile again. And again without the warning. It really was unfair. 'Apparently, emotional upset can cause things to go…backwards… in that department,' he added. 'So Toni put her in a nappy. I think Mollie just got confused.'

Jennie frowned. 'So… it's safe to say that nappies don't go down the toilet. The question is: what *do* you do with them?'

He looked heavenwards. 'I'm thinking a nuclear device of some sort wouldn't be out of place.'

Jennie laughed out loud, then clapped a hand over her mouth, realising the sleeping Mollie was only a few feet from the open bathroom door. Alex's eyes twinkled. And right then, covered in smears of stuff she'd rather not identify and looking as if she'd wrestled with a tornado, Jennie started to fall in love with her husband all over again.

CHAPTER EIGHT

ALEX didn't think he'd ever seen Jennie look so beautiful. But, while his hibernating heart had started to beat again, he didn't need to get ahead of himself. Things had changed. Big things.

He let his smile fade and caught her gaze. 'We need to talk.'

She nodded, her own smile slipping, and when it was gone he felt awful for putting that look of sadness in her eyes.

They crept past Mollie's sleeping form, curled into one corner of his bed.

'Do you think she's going to be all right like that?' he whispered to Jennie. 'What if she falls out?'

Jennie shrugged and motioned for him to come outside. They both stood in the doorway and watched the little lump under the duvet breathe in and out. 'Where has she been sleeping up until now?' she said in a hushed voice.

'At my parents',' he replied. 'I've been staying with them for the last couple of weeks. I had things to do… A funeral to arrange. I thought it would be better to let her get to know them and be comfortable with them, and then when I had to shoot off, she wouldn't feel abandoned.'

Jennie gave a little nod, and he was glad his decision had made sense to her.

'Toni and her boys have been around a lot over Christmas, so she offered to look after Mollie today while Mum and Dad went to a friend's birthday dinner, and then bring her home to me this evening.'

Mollie stirred and they both froze. Once they were sure she wasn't going to wake up and wail, he put a finger to his lips and closed the bedroom door slowly and quietly. Not wanting to go too far, just in case Mollie did fall out of bed, he sat down on the landing with his back against the bedroom wall. Jennie gave a what-the-hell kind of gesture with her hands and followed suit.

She twisted to look at the blank wall behind them. 'Do you think she's going to be okay?'

'I hope so.'

Things had to get better from here on, didn't they? They had to. Because he had the awful feeling that he was Mollie's last hope, that it was up to him now to provide what she needed and keep her safe.

Jennie turned back and slumped against the wall. 'Me, too.'

Unexpected warmth flickered in his chest. It had been easy to think of Jennie as shallow and selfish when he'd been angry with her. Anger that really should have been directed elsewhere. At another wife who'd disappeared and taken his dreams with her. A wife who'd robbed him of the first three years of his daughter's life. Who'd left him in this hellish limbo.

Jennie's sudden disappearance had brought that awful sense of dread back, as fresh and new and raw as the day Becky had left. Maybe he'd waited longer than he should have to go and find Jennie. Maybe he'd waited until after Christmas because he'd wanted her to stew, to feel some of what he'd been feeling. He'd reasoned that Mollie was his top priority, that Jennie had made it quite clear she didn't want to be with him. It struck him now that it was possible that a tiny part of him had wanted to punish her, because having control for once—being able to decide when and where they'd see each other again—had felt good. It had been wrong of him.

He shook his head and looked at his wife. No, Jennie wasn't selfish or shallow. Impulsive, maybe. Spontaneous. Warm. Fun. All the things he'd forgotten how to be.

He glanced in the direction of the bedroom again. 'I think we'll be okay,' he said, more to himself than to Jennie.

At least he'd almost convinced himself of this. And he would have been successful, but for the fact that, since he'd brought her home, Mollie shrank into herself if he tried to touch her now. Maybe he reminded her of the sadness she'd felt that day. Who knew? But things would improve. Mollie had been through a very traumatic experience and he just needed to be patient.

He hadn't noticed the silence stretching until Jennie said, 'Ear-splitting cries and nappy emergencies aside, she seems an adorable little girl.' They both stared at the banisters and the quiet turned uncomfortable and jagged.

They were back to this, then. Polite comments and folded hands, when only minutes ago it had all been so different.

Every day with Jennie was a roller coaster. He'd

realised that soon after he'd first met her. He just hadn't realised that the lows would include this sense of distance, all the things still unsaid piling up between them. At the beginning of their relationship, the roller coaster had been exciting, all-consuming, leaving him breathless and in the moment, blocking out everything that tormented him. Jennie had been just what he'd needed.

But instead of continuing to ride high in Jennie's adrenalin-fuelled world, he'd dragged her down into his reality. Now the lows of their ride weren't merely rest periods before the next leg of the adventure, they were deep, dark pits. And it wasn't over yet. They had plenty more hills and valleys to conquer—if she decided to stick around, of course.

'What are you going to tell her about us? About *me?*' Jennie said.

'I don't know.'

Silence followed. Well, not exactly silence; no words were uttered, but Jennie fidgeted and shifted.

'She's gone through enough, had enough uncertainty. I had meant to tell you about her before I introduced the pair of you. I didn't want to confuse her if you weren't willing to try again.' He turned to look at her. 'I know this is complicated...'

The fidgeting stopped and she returned his gaze. Normally, she would have quipped about his gift for understatement, but she merely stared at him, her eyes large and pale.

'I want a future with you, Jennie. We made promises to each other, including "for better or worse". It's up to you how I introduce you to Mollie.' He took a deep breath, asked the question they'd both sidestepped all day. 'Are you willing to give us a go?'

He couldn't help but notice how she looked away when he said 'us'. He didn't blame her. *Us* was no longer just the two of them. He'd changed the rules behind her back. When they'd made their promises, they both hadn't known all the facts.

He had to give her the chance to decide afresh, he suddenly realised. A chance to opt in with her eyes open, knowing everything there was to know.

She hadn't answered him yet. Her bottom lip was clenched between her teeth and she was frowning, looking so pained and torn. He wanted to reach forward and smooth the ridges in her forehead flat, to kiss the indecision from her face, but he was afraid she would mimic Mollie and shrink away from him.

'I know this isn't what you signed up for when you said "I do",' he added. 'I'm sorry.'

He wished she'd smile. Say something. But she looked...empty. She reflected nothing back to him now.

Jennie drew in a breath and held it. 'I think I need some more of that fresh air,' she announced, and stood up. 'I'm going for a walk.'

He watched her walk down the stairs, and then he got up and followed her. From the study window he watched her walk down the drive, arms clamped across her coat, holding herself together, and only when she'd disappeared completely did he move.

He stepped back and his foot made a watery noise on the carpet.

The coffee. He'd totally forgotten about the coffee.

There was a pool of dark liquid on the carpet at one side of his desk. It was an awful mess. His mess. His responsibility.

Jennie didn't pay much attention to where she was going, which was a pity because the village of Elmhurst was beautiful on this clear January day. The blades of grass on the verges were crisp and razor-sharp, only just having shed their jackets of frost. The sky was a luminous baby-blue and even the brown furrows of the fields in the distance looked pretty.

She kept walking until she saw the village church, a quaint little Norman building nestled beside the vast hedge of the neighbouring stately home. Her watch told her she was too late to catch the service, but one of the doors was open and she suddenly craved the lonely, peaceful feeling always to be found in empty churches. Perhaps a sense of calm from the recent prayers would still be lingering. Perhaps she could borrow a bit of that peace for herself, so she could start to sort and label her jostling thoughts.

The lights were still on inside and a few candles were lit. Far from looking grey and gloomy, the interior of the little church was warm and welcoming. Jennie ducked inside and slid her bottom along one of the back pews until she was resting on the far side of a tall sculpted pillar.

Where did she start?

Her missing groom? His secret daughter? The off-the-rails ex-wife? It was all so confusing.

Start with how you feel.

The thought that interrupted her mental ramblings was calm and clear. Precise. She liked that. Needed that. She latched on to it.

I love Alex.

She didn't say it out loud, but she felt as if she had. She did love Alex—despite the hastiness of their marriage, despite all the stupid things they'd both done since then. Her heart told her he was still the man she'd fallen in love with, and she was inclined to believe it. It was just this version of Alex was more…three-dimensional. He was no longer the tall, dark stranger who had swept her off her feet and into his arms, who had surprised her with his intensity and passion. He was a father. And she'd glimpsed some of the hidden depths she'd always half-known were there inside him.

She loved Alex, and she wanted to stay with him.

There. She was getting somewhere now, building on that original thought. She decided to keep going.

She imagined him back at his house, frowning out of the study window, or bending over Mollie in the kitchen, carefully tasting her cakes before bestowing his economical, but nonetheless heart-felt, approval.

The picture in her head wasn't the future she'd said yes to in that gaudy little chapel in Vegas. Her own ideas about what life with Alex would be like were slightly fuzzy, it had to be said, but they had been a comfortable fit. This new picture of how her life might unfold felt foreign—as if she were trying on someone else's clothes.

Was it horrible of her to falter at the idea of becoming an instant mother, of bringing up another woman's child?

She decided it *was* horrible. Understandable, though. She leaned back and looked up at the vaulted ceiling of the church. The curves and arches seemed to go on for ever, each joining and merging with the next to form an elegant pattern. This place asked for honesty, and she knew beyond a shadow of a doubt that it was better to admit to her less-than-glittering feelings than to whitewash them with the things she thought she *should* feel. This was the rest of her life she was making a decision about—and she'd played too many games, taken too many chances with it already.

Alex needs me.

Another thought. Fact. Whatever it was…

But that statement wasn't as simple as it seemed. Why did he need her? What for? She'd assumed he'd needed *her* when he'd looked into her eyes and said his wedding vows, but was it her soul Alex craved or did he need her for the vacancy of 'wife and mother'? Someone to fill the hole another woman had left behind.

Mother. That was not a label most people would attach to her easily, believing she was still clinging to the last vestiges of her own childhood. What if they were right? What if she didn't have it in her? She'd always liked to believe that she'd make a wonderful mother, but there was a half-grown specimen back in Alex's house. Imagining a hazy future with a tiny pink newborn wrapped in a fleecy blanket wasn't the same thing as being asked to step into the role of parent right this moment.

And what about Mollie? What if she made things worse for the child with her clumsy attempts at being a stepmother?

She grimaced at her own thoughts. Never in her life had she ever imagined herself as a *step-mother*. They were a different brand of woman. But then she thought of Marion, thought of how tough it must have been for her to take on a wilful girl still grieving for her lost mother. She thought of Marion's patience and grace, and wished fervently that DNA could jump the gap left by the lack of their blood relationship.

The truth was she had no idea if she could be a good mother. But how did anyone know what the future held? If everyone cowered away from the unknown, what a miserable place the world would be. She would never have married Alex if she'd thought that way. But married him she had, because it had felt right at the time. It still felt right.

Alex needed her and she wasn't going to let him down, mainly because she suspected he needed her more even than he realised. And she needed him. The only way to make things work now was to jump in with both feet as she usually did and give it all she had.

This might not be the future she'd envisioned when she'd joined her life to Alex's, but she was tired of running away, being the irresponsible, flighty party girl. She could change. She could. That was why she was going to ignore the whispers in her head that told her she wasn't ready for this, that she should think of herself and leave while she had the chance.

She thought back to their wedding day, saw herself standing opposite him in her oyster satin vintage dress. Someone else's dress, but it had been a perfect fit. Who was to say she couldn't slide into the life that had originally been fashioned for someone else as easily? Let's face it, she thought, I could hardly do a worse job than the first candidate, and I'm the girl who's supposed to be up for anything.

She looked down at the charm bracelet on her right wrist. Slowly, she unhooked it and removed the gold band. It had always looked out of place there. She laid it on the pew while she did her bracelet up again, and then, with a solemnity that matched her surroundings, she slid her wedding ring back onto her left hand.

Meet me in The White Hart? Half an hour, was all Jennie's text message had said. Alex had almost texted back, saying he couldn't leave Mollie—Jennie should have realised that—but then he'd reasoned that it might be better to meet on neutral territory. Mollie didn't need to hear any more hushed conversations, thick with tension, so he'd rushed next door and persuaded the nice old lady to come in and babysit.

The local pub was fairly full when he got there, lots of people taking advantage of the lull after Christmas and New Year to grab a pub lunch or a few beers with friends. In a few days life would gear up again—the commuter trains would be standing-room only, the roads clogged in the mornings, offices full of unwilling workers—but for now a sense of calm had descended over the nation, and everyone seemed happy and relaxed.

Jennie was tucked away in a corner of the pub, as far from the jovial crowd as she could position herself, sipping a coffee and looking nervous. That shocked him. His Jennie never shrank back from anything, never looked all meek and mouse-like.

Even though a bite of food hadn't passed his lips that morning, he suddenly felt as if he'd had rocks for breakfast. He crossed the pub lounge, dodging through tightly arranged wooden chairs and tables, and his heart began to thud uncomfortably under his jumper.

She was sitting on an upholstered bench that curved round one of the corners of the room and he slid in beside her, startling her. She'd been talking on her mobile and he caught the end of the conversation—something about being back in London soon—and the rocks inside him grew in density.

Jennie slid her phone closed and set it on the table next to her coffee cup, then she gave him a weak smile.

'So, you've made your choice,' he said tonelessly.

'Yes.' She fiddled with her coffee cup, turning it this way, then that on its saucer.

'Back to London,' he said, all the time looking at her phone. 'Back to your life.'

At that she started. 'No! I mean…yes…back to my life, but not…'

And then he saw a flash of gold as she twirled her cup again. On her left hand.

'…not like that. My life is with you, Alex. I only need to go back up to town to get more clothes, my things.'

Just like that, the rocks crumbled into dust. No, *melted away,* leaving him feeling not just warm but so full of heat and fire inside he could barely contain it. He didn't think about it, didn't plan it; he just reached for Jennie and kissed her, forgetting completely where he was and who might be watching, just as he had on the night he'd first met her.

She was the first to pull away, blushing. 'Alex… people can see us.'

'Don't care,' he said, staring into her eyes and refusing to let her look away.

She'd given him something precious in her answer. Hope. For the first time in weeks—years, maybe—he started to truly believe life might start going right again, that the future might not be as desolate as he'd begun to think it would be.

Jennie smiled at him, and it had an added dimension from her usual cheeky, devil-may-care smirk. It was warm and wavering and vulnerable. He felt himself lean forward again, but she halted him with a raised palm on his chest.

'We need to talk.'

He nodded. This was no way to behave. Trouble was, Jennie always made him feel this way. It was why she was so intoxicating. He forgot everything else, existed only in the present, just as she did.

He caught the eye of one of the barmaids and ordered a couple more coffees.

'I've been thinking while I've been sitting here,' Jennie said. 'I don't know much about kids, and I wouldn't presume to tell you what to do where Mollie is concerned, but I don't want my arrival in your life to cause her even more upset.'

'I know. But what's the alternative? I can't pretend you don't exist, that we never married.'

She looked thoughtful. 'Maybe it would be better if I wasn't on the scene for a while—just until she's more settled.'

Alex reached for Jennie's left hand, took it in his and kissed the knuckle closest to the gold ring. His ring. He loved her for suggesting this, but it wouldn't do.

'No, I don't want that. We're a family now. We stick together.'

She clamped her hand over the top of his and squeezed. Ploughing through this nightmare with Jennie by his side made it seem doable.

'I'd rather we faced this now, while everything's new, rather than spring another surprise on her later.' If there was one thing he'd learned from his time with Jennie, it was that you couldn't run from relationships. They were always there, in the background, changing and evolving, even if you thought nothing was going on.

'I have an idea. A compromise,' Jennie said slowly, and Alex realised he'd been lost in thought and that a steaming cup of black coffee now sat in front of him on the table and he had no idea where it had come from.

'A compromise?'

She nodded, suddenly looking much more determined. 'Perhaps it would be better if I went ho—' She caught herself, substituted another word. 'If I went back to my flat tonight. Maybe even for an extra day. It would give me a chance to pack properly...break the news to my family...'

She broke off and winced, rolled her eyes, and he brightened further. This was the game-for-anything Jennie he knew he could count on.

'And it would give you an opportunity to prepare Mollie, tell her about me instead of me just invading her new life with her father without any warning.'

He drank some of his coffee and considered Jennie's suggestion, turning it over in his mind, looking at the shape of it from every angle. The last thing he wanted was to spend more time away from Jennie, for her to leave this evening. His bed felt empty enough as it was. Tonight it would feel like a football pitch if she wasn't beside him in it. But he had to admit she was making sense.

'Come back with me now,' he countered. 'Stay for lunch. Stay for the afternoon, and then I'll drive you back to London myself. You can start to get to know Mollie.'

Armed with four suitcases, three garment bags and half a ton of advice from her stepmother buzzing around inside her head, Jennie left her flat two days later. She'd been desperate to see Alex again—counting the minutes—but now he was here, collecting the first of the cases and hauling them down to his car, and everything felt…rehearsed, as if she were practising for the real thing and this was only marking time. They were doing all the right things, saying all the right things, but it was as if, during the night, someone had reached inside her and switched her emotions off. But that didn't stop the doubts pecking away at her consciousness.

Had he changed his mind? Was he having second thoughts? She wasn't equipped to deal with the role she was about to take on and she knew it. Perhaps Alex did, too.

Once inside Alex's car, she settled into the

seat and closed her eyes, letting him navigate the busy London streets without interruption or interference.

Where was all the heat and passion and momentum from the early days of their marriage? They stumbled upon it sometimes, knocking themselves flat with the force of it, but at other times, like today, it was as if they were mechanically going through the motions.

Was this what marriage was supposed to be like? She'd always thought it would be cosy and comfortable—dull, even. She hadn't expected this confusing switching from hot to cold, and she had no control over when it happened.

It wasn't until the traffic noise dulled and the roads became longer and straighter that Alex spoke. 'I'm named as the father on Mollie's birth certificate,' he said without taking his eyes off the road.

She glanced at him. 'That was quick!'

'I got a phone call on the way up to you,' he said, 'but I'm not sure it's changed anything.'

'It has to be a relief, even just a little bit,' she said.

He did a sideways nod that managed to contradict itself.

'You think Becky might have lied?'

Another nod. 'I've decided to have the DNA test done anyway. We'll get the results in a couple of weeks, hopefully.' He breathed out. 'Neither of us needs to have a question mark hanging over our heads.'

Jennie was just about to say she'd be happy to wait if he was, but then she realised the 'us' he was talking about was him and his daughter. She wasn't included.

They'd talked quite a few times over the last couple of days about Mollie, and these phone conversations had also been something new. Now, they both frowned as they spoke, their heads full of strategies and backup plans, the total focus on Mollie. No more whispered promises that made her insides heat. No more excited plotting about the next bit of snatched time together. Perhaps, now she'd be installed in his house and they could see each other whenever they wanted, it wouldn't be exciting like that any more, and she wasn't sure she liked that. Knowing Alex had charged out of his office early to meet her, or had stayed up all night clearing his desk so he could meet her for lunch had made her feel special. She didn't want their private time together to be reduced to something routine and functional. Where was the fun in that?

She closed her eyes again and, Alex being Alex, he didn't press her for a response to his statement. Never had she been more grateful for his dislike of extraneous words.

Her muscles were bunched tight and she sighed and tried to relax them. There was another thing preying on her mind. And the more she tried *not* to think about it, the bigger and scarier it grew.

She was very aware of the fact that she and Alex hadn't…that there hadn't been a chance to be alone and…

This was ridiculous! She was even avoiding thinking the word! This wasn't like her at all.

Sex.

There. She'd allowed it to the front of her consciousness, said it mentally aloud. They hadn't had sex since they'd decided to patch their tattered marriage back together, and she was suddenly very nervous about the whole thing and she didn't know why. It was just sex. No big deal. Only…

What if that was all new and different, too?

Oh, it would be fine if they were all hot and steamy and in the moment, as they had been on their honeymoon. More than fine, actually. But, in the last few days, she'd become painfully aware that 'moments' were fleeting things, and she and Alex didn't always find themselves slap-bang in the middle of one any more.

But she didn't have too long to work herself into knots about the matter because the car slowed and she opened her lids to find they were crawling down Alex's drive. Well, *her* drive now.

Her stomach hollowed out. This was it. Her first day as a mother. Lord help that poor child.

Poor child, my foot.

'Hang on a second, Lucy. I just need to…'

Jennie pressed her mobile phone to her chest, marched across the room and rescued the TV remote from the floor. She punched the volume button repeatedly. Who could think with cartoons blaring at an ear-splitting level?

'Mollie?' Jennie said sweetly. 'Leave the volume alone, okay?'

Was the child deaf? She certainly didn't react to Jennie's plea, just kept staring at the jumble of noise and colour on the screen, and as soon as Jennie walked back to her laptop, balanced on the arm of the sofa, Mollie sidled up to the set and left her finger on the button.

Jennie peeled the phone from her chest and put it to her ear. 'Listen, Lucy, I can't talk now. Just go ahead and book The Savoy. I'll sweet-talk the client into thinking it's the best decision he ever made.'

She slid her phone closed and looked at Mollie, engrossed in the colourful antics on the television. Did the girl have hearing problems? Jennie sat on the arm of the sofa and folded her arms across her chest.

'Cookies,' she whispered.

Mollie glanced in her direction, looking hopeful.

Yup. Just as she'd thought. Hearing fine; disposition awkward.

Jennie slid down the arm of the sofa into the seat and reached over to shut her laptop. Working from home had seemed such a simple solution to their current dilemma. Alex was due in court this week and while they were in the process of hiring a nanny to help with the childcare, Jennie had volunteered to stay at home and look after Mollie. It was only day two and she was ready to run screaming from the house.

How did parents cope with this full-time? How did they not go insane? Back at her flat last week, when she hadn't been packing up her single girl life, she'd spent huge chunks of time reading a highly recommended parenting book. Crash course, if you like. But she didn't feel in the least equipped to deal with a three-year-old who thought she was the boss.

How did mothers learn to deal with this kind of thing? Perhaps there was a secret technique they divulged in hallowed whispers at childbirth classes. Minor problem: Jennie hadn't done any childbirth classes because she'd come to motherhood the same way she came to everything else—feet first and out of order—and it wasn't making it even the tiniest bit easier.

She thought of some of her cousins who'd brought their little darlings to Alice and Cameron's wedding, about how the children had run riot and the parents had large dark circles under their eyes and a perpetually harried look, and she started to get even more scared. Perhaps it never got better. Maybe this what her life was going to be like from now on. For ever. She shivered.

Distraction.

That was something she remembered from the

book. Okay, Mollie wasn't having a tantrum, but maybe if she suggested doing something different, something exciting, her stepdaughter might allow her to use the off button on the TV set.

Jennie went and stood in front of the television and earned herself a scowl from Mollie. 'How about we go out?' she said brightly.

The intense look of concentration on Mollie's face as she pondered Jennie's suggestion was actually quite cute. She scrunched up her forehead and looked at the carpet. Eventually she looked up and said, 'Can we go and see Mummy? Is she still sleeping?'

This wasn't the first time she'd heard a question like this in the last forty-eight hours. Evidently some bright spark in Alex's family had decided to explain death to Mollie as a really long sleep. Jennie hadn't wanted to upset the little girl by being blunt, so she'd just fudged it when she'd had to answer this question. And she had no idea what else people had said to Mollie about her mother's death. The poor kid was confused enough as it was; Jennie didn't want to add to that.

'I thought we might go to the park. Does that sound like a fun thing to do?'

Mollie nodded, but her shoulders slumped forward. Jennie reasoned she'd feel better once she was on a swing or something. There was something about swings that always left you smiling and breathless.

Fifteen minutes later, they were both bundled up in hats, scarves and gloves and were at the park just down the road from Alex's house. Jennie stamped her feet and clapped her hands together as she watched Mollie wear the slide to a shine.

They were the only ones in the park. But damp January afternoons weren't always a favourite time to come and play. It hadn't actually rained yet today, but the clouds hung low in the sky and Jennie could feel their moisture on her cheeks. It wouldn't be long.

Mollie seemed happy enough now. Jennie's 'distraction' seemed to have worked. Mollie moved on to the roundabout and sat talking to herself on the edge while she pushed at the ground with both feet to spin herself round slowly.

'Do you want me to make it go faster?' Jennie called over.

Mollie glanced up and shook her head, so Jennie decided to keep an eye on her from the swings.

She sat down on the nearest one and used the toe of her boot to give her a bit of movement.

The swing had been the place where Jennie had done all her hard thinking when she'd been a child. There was something about the way the air blew past you, backwards and forwards, about the way you seemed to fly above the ground, that made it easy to get things straight in your head.

Mollie was still chattering away, but she had taken her hat off. Jennie thought about asking her to put it back on, but decided the kid deserved a break. She put both feet on the floor and pushed a little harder, used her legs to work up more of a decent swing.

What was she going to do about Alex? They'd shared a bed for the last two nights and she'd been waiting for him to give her a signal that he'd prefer it if they did more than just snore in it, but he hadn't. They'd kissed—quite a few times— and everything had seemed great, but he always pulled back before it developed into something more. Why was that? Couldn't he bring himself to…? Had she hurt him that much when she'd run away from him?

The rhythm of the swing was soothing. The wind pushed her hair round her face then sucked it away again, over and over, and as the ground moved past more quickly, the swing began to do its magic.

She knew Alex wasn't punishing her—he wasn't that vindictive, and it went against his noble nature, but she couldn't fathom why...

His noble nature. That was it!

Alex wasn't avoiding her. He was waiting for her. She breathed a sigh of relief. How could she not have seen it before? He was being patient with her, waiting for her to show him she was ready. She wished that he'd have talked to her about it, but she was starting to understand that just wasn't his style.

Maybe tonight...after they'd put Mollie to bed.

She looked out at the horizon and smiled. The sky had turned a lovely shade of blueish-purple, which meant sunset wasn't far away. She jumped lightly off the swing onto the bouncy surface beneath and stood up straight. It was time to get home.

She put her hands on her hips and looked over to the roundabout. All she could see was a turquoise woolly hat, circuiting slowly. She scanned the rest of the playground, regretting the fact she'd left it so long before she'd decided to return home. The shadows of the bushes and trees, which hadn't seemed particularly dark a few minutes earlier, were now blending and blurring, making it difficult to make out Mollie's navy coat.

She took a few steps forward, studied the slide, the climbing frame. And then it hit her.

Mollie was gone.

CHAPTER NINE

A SHAKY panic gripped Jennie, causing her stomach to spasm. She spun around, eyes darting this way and that, desperate to be wrong, but the park was empty.

She had no idea what to do. Absolutely no idea.

Blindly, she reached into her pocket for her mobile phone and was just about to press the button to dial Alex's number when she paused. This was the last thing Alex wanted to hear—that the daughter he'd only just found was lost. *And that* you *lost her,* a little voice whispered harshly in her ear. *It's your fault. He'll never forgive you for it.*

Jennie's heart sank even further. Despite her instinct for self-preservation, she decided she couldn't *not* tell Alex, but she also reasoned that Mollie had only been missing for a matter of minutes. She might have wandered into the bushes or be hiding. Before she rang Alex and passed the fear on, she was going to make sure it was a genuine emergency.

She ran around the whole playground, checking behind every over-sized frog-shaped bin, in the little house in the jungle gym, behind every piece of play equipment.

Nothing.

Mollie wasn't here. Either that or she was *way* better at hide-and-seek than Jennie had ever been.

Her phone burned in her pocket. Five minutes, she told herself. She'd check the surrounding area first. Perhaps Mollie had strayed to say hello to a friendly-looking dog, or got talking to someone…

Even fiercer chills ran up and down her body.

She dashed over to the nearest clump of trees and bushes and dived in, only to emerge empty-handed—bar a multitude of twigs in her hair and something unpleasant-smelling on her boot. She wiped it off on the damp grass and carried on searching. It took more than five minutes to do a complete sweep of the area, but she ignored that fact. Twilight had fallen. It would be completely dark in less than half an hour. Jennie wished fervently that she had something as useful as a mini torch on her key ring, but it was adorned only with sparkly little shoes and a chunky silver letter J.

It was cold and dark. She shouldn't be out here. Mollie shouldn't be out here. They should be watching deafening cartoons, sitting on the living room floor and eating cookies, waiting for Alex to come home.

Home…

Jennie held her breath.

Would Mollie have gone home? What if she'd merely wandered off and then had returned to the playground, only to find no sight of Jennie because she'd been searching the bushes? She was a bright kid, and Alex's house was visible from the playground. Would she have taken herself off home?

Jennie started running.

Her cold breath seemed to be ripping shreds out of her lungs by the time she reached Alex's house. Jennie had her key in the lock as soon as she could unknot her fingers. She slammed it open.

'Mollie?' she yelled. 'Mollie!'

She made herself stay still and wait for a response. As she stood there, panting, her brain caught up with her surroundings. There were no lights on anywhere. Everything was just as they'd left it.

'Mollie?' Her voice was quieter now. She knew she wouldn't get an answer but she started walking around, opening doors, flipping light switches, looking in corners and behind bits of furniture. And when she'd covered the whole of the ground floor, she went upstairs and repeated the process.

Nothing. No sign of Mollie.

She was going to have to phone Alex.

Mollie's bedroom had been the first place she'd checked up here, and she returned there now, wandering over to the large window and cooling her forehead on the glass as she stared into the back garden. There was no putting it off now. She reached into her pocket and dialled his number, her stomach icing over. Coward that she was, she hoped fervently that it'd go to voicemail. No such luck.

'Hi, what's up?' He sounded distracted, as if he was reading something. Nothing like the low-voiced, sexy greetings he used to give her before they were married.

Jennie closed her eyes. 'It's Mollie.'

His voice changed instantly. 'What's happened?' She had no doubt she had his full attention now.

'I…I can't find her. We were at the park and she ran off.'

There was an ominous silence on the other end of the line. Alex must be furious with her. Two days and she'd failed at being a mother. It made her pitiful attempt at being a good wife look stellar in comparison.

'Where have you looked?'

She banged her head against the glass. 'Everywhere! I don't know what to do.'

Why? Why had Mollie run away? Why today? Was there something Jennie had missed? Something she'd done wrong?

Suddenly, an image of another girl popped into her mind. A little blonde girl with a blue suitcase clutched in her hand, scurrying away from her house, looking over her shoulder to see if anyone was following her.

Wow. Where had that memory come from?

Running away had been a favourite game of Jennie's when she'd been a child. She'd pack her bunny and her favourite book and a bag of toffees, just in case, in the little blue case she kept her ballet kit in, and she'd hide herself away somewhere in the vast gardens of her father's house. Usually, the pool house. Maybe the gazebo in summer.

Okay, it hadn't exactly been a *game*. She truly had been unhappy in those moments. But the running away had been more about wanting to be found again, knowing that someone cared enough to notice she was missing, cared enough to come and find her. A silly, childish tactic to demand her father prove his love.

She knew now that her father had loved her the best he could, that he'd struggled with his own grief after her mother's death, just hadn't known what to do with a wilful little tearaway who wanted everything he had to give and more. He'd tried. But it had been easier for him to spoil her with *things* rather than attention, something she'd loved and hated at the same time. Maybe it had been easier for him to do that than spend time with the person who reminded him the most of everything he'd lost.

A single tear slid down her face. More often than not, she'd had a long wait out in the pool house. Many times she'd crept back in the house at nightfall, tired and hungry, and had crawled under her duvet and lay there, shivering.

She pulled her forehead off the window and straightened. A blob in the dark garden suddenly became recognisable—the tree house. Well, not so much a tree house as a play house on stilts, built up against a large horse chestnut tree, with a small veranda at the front with wooden steps leading down to the lawn. There was one place she hadn't checked. Somewhere Mollie might have gone if all the doors were locked.

'Hold on, Alex. I've had an idea.'

Jennie was at the top of the stairs by the time she finished talking. She didn't know where the key to the French windows in the lounge was, so she ran out of the back door and round the side of the house. The lawn was soft and muddy, but she didn't slow until she was standing at the bottom of the steps that led up to the little wooden house.

'Jennie?' Alex's voice was harsh in her ear.

Was she kidding herself? Was this just wishful thinking? She stood still, listening for any creak, trying to decipher any movement in the shadows inside the tree house.

'Jennie!'

She couldn't seem to answer him, her voice

stolen by sheer panic. The wind rustled the bare branches up above her head and cooled her cheeks. In the distance, a car rumbled along the road to the village centre. Her heart thumped.

And then...

The shades of grey inside the tree house shifted. Or had she just been standing here, staring at that little Perspex window for too long? She ran up the five low steps to the veranda. She stooped to open the half-sized door and stuck her head inside. There was a scrabbling noise—please, don't let it be a rat!—and then silence.

She was too nervous to do much more than croak. 'Mollie?'

More scrabbling. 'Go away!'

A flood of endorphins hit Jennie so hard she almost fell over. She compromised by crumpling onto the floor and edging a little closer to where she *thought* the shuffling had come from.

'It's okay,' she said to Alex. 'I've found her.' And then she slid her phone closed, too intent on finding out if her stepdaughter was all right to worry about Alex. He'd have plenty of time to shout at her later.

'I was worried about you,' she said softly.

The only answer she got was a sniff.

'What are you doing out here?'

'Looking for Mummy.'

The answer cracked Jennie's heart wide open. 'Oh, darling. Why did you think she'd be in here?'

'Auntie Toni said I lost Mummy. And she said Mummy would always be with me. So I 'cided to look in here, just in case. I found Daddy's torch but it not work.'

Jennie closed her eyes, despite the dark. She remembered this. The way grown-ups talked to you about death. Some of her relatives had said some very confusing things after her mother had died, and it had taken her quite a while to come to grips with everything. However, she'd been eight when her mother had died. Mollie was only three. She probably didn't even understand what it meant, how final it was. And having adults talking in hushed voices and vague terms was only making matters worse.

'Mollie, do you have Daddy's torch there? Can I have a look at it?'

She heard more shuffling and then heard something roll along the wooden floor before it hit her ankle. She fumbled with the rubber casing until she found the button. The torch was old and it took a push harder than a three-year-old's thumb would manage. A pale yellow circle lit the floor. Jennie put the torch in her lap, facing away from both their faces and looked at Mollie. She was huddled up in the corner, her lashes thick with tears and her nose slimy.

'Are you cold? Do you want to sit on my lap?'

Mollie shook her head, but she inched a little closer.

Jennie took a deep breath. She might be doing totally the wrong thing here, but there wasn't time to rush inside and thumb through her parenting book. She was just going to have to go with her gut. All she'd wanted when her own mother had died was for someone to sit down and talk to her about it. But nobody had. They'd pretended nothing had happened and tried to be happy around her. They'd clothed everything in euphemisms rather than giving her facts. And it had made her sad that no one would let her talk about her mummy, about how much she missed her and how sad she was.

Without warning, her eyes filled with tears. She blinked them away.

She looked Mollie in the eye. 'When I was a

little girl my mummy died, too,' she said, watching her stepdaughter's face and trying to gauge her reaction. Mollie went very still and looked at her with wide eyes.

'Did you ever find your mummy 'gain? Did you lose her, too?'

Jennie swallowed. 'No, sweetheart. I didn't.' And she went on to explain, with simple words and plain facts, why she wouldn't see her mother again—not on this earth, anyway.

Mollie's lips began to wobble. Jennie saw the look of hope in Mollie's eyes, begging her to tell her what she'd just pieced together wasn't true, and it took all her willpower not to hide that truth in platitudes, the way everyone else had done for Mollie. The little girl's whole face crumpled up. 'Don't want Mummy to be dead,' she whispered.

I don't want mine to be dead either, Jennie thought. And I miss her so much. One of the tears she thought she'd dealt with escaped and rolled down her cheek. She saw Mollie watch it, a look of surprise on her little round features.

'Why are you crying?' she said, sniffing, tears falling fast down her own cheeks.

Jennie found she needed to sniff, too. 'Because

I'm sad my mummy's gone, too,' she said. 'And sometimes I get angry. But it's okay to feel like that. It's okay to be angry or sad or happy or fed up, and it's okay to cry if you need to.'

Mollie crawled towards her and inspected her tears with chubby, inquisitive fingers.

'Are you sure you're not cold?' Jennie said, trying to smile. 'Because I am, and my lap desperately needs warming up.'

Mollie blinked and then she climbed into Jennie's lap and put her arms around her. And then she rubbed Jennie's back with a tiny hand in a way Becky must have done to soothe her when she was upset. That just made Jennie cry all the harder. All of Mollie's defences crumbled and she clutched on to Jennie and sobbed. Jennie wasn't in much of a position to do anything but join her.

After a short while she felt Mollie relax in her arms. Jennie wiped her own cheeks with her fingers, not even bothering to avoid her mascara.

'I don't know about you, but I need a tissue.'

A little head nodded against her chest, and Jennie decided not to think about what kind of smears were now on her rather expensive designer jumper.

'And I'm hungry, too,' she added. 'How about we go inside and find something to eat?'

Another nod.

She carefully lifted Mollie off her lap and scrambled to her feet. 'Why don't you use the torch?' she said to Mollie, who brightened instantly. As she stood up and brushed the dust off her rear end, Jennie thought of yesterday's attempt at tea—burnt toast, lukewarm baked beans...

She backed out of the tree house door, stooping to avoid whacking her head on the top of the frame. 'Stuff it,' she mumbled to herself. 'I'm getting takeaway.'

Her boot squelched in the mud at the bottom of the steps as a little voice called out from behind her, 'Can we have pizza?'

She smiled and held out a hand. 'Of course.'

Jennie stared at the open pizza box, having nothing better to do than watch the remaining slices get harder and curlier. Alex hadn't said much when he'd come in. He'd just dropped his briefcase and coat in the hall and quietly climbed the stairs to Mollie's bedroom. He'd been up there forty-five minutes now.

She decided she'd go crazy if she didn't find something to do, so she started to clear the dishes. She was just putting the last one into the dishwasher when she heard Alex's footsteps in the hall. Her mind filled with reasons why this wasn't her fault, why he shouldn't be angry with her. That also was stupid. Suddenly she felt Mollie's age, scared with the same chilly fear that she'd had when her father had made one of his rare appearances in her bedroom. Scared of what he'd say. Because whenever there was trouble, she was sure to be the cause of it.

But Alex didn't rant and rave. He didn't say a thing. Didn't look at her with that heavy disapproval in his eyes. And maybe that was worse. He collected a pair of wine glasses from the cupboard, filled them with Merlot and gestured in the direction of the living room. Jennie followed him there.

They sat in different chairs—Jennie by the fire, Alex on the sofa—the cool awkwardness between them preventing them from doing anything else. So much for tonight being The Night. Jennie sipped her wine and stared into the fire while he collected his thoughts, found a way to let whatever difficult words were in him out. But it took a lot longer than she expected. Alex was so quiet, so still, it made her feel fidgety. Pretty soon she was screaming inside her head.

And then it all came spilling out of her. 'I'm so sorry,' she said. 'I only took my eyes off her for a moment...'

He shot her words down with a look. A what-do-you-think-you-were-doing kind of look. She waited for him to say it—to tell her she was a failure and that he'd made a mistake when he'd asked her to stay.

'Mollie was almost asleep when I got up there.' A pained look crossed his face, and he looked as if he was going to say something. After a few seconds of silence, his jaw hardened.

'Is she okay?' Jennie asked quietly.

Alex nodded. 'I just sat in the armchair and watched her until she fell asleep.'

Jennie pressed her lips together and tried to smile at him. It came out all wonky. What could she say? What could *anyone* say to make this right?

Alex looked deep into his wine glass. He hadn't even touched it yet. 'I don't think I could bear it if we do the DNA test and the results come back negative.'

Jennie swallowed as Alex's eyes shimmered in the firelight. So that was why he'd stalled on getting it done. She bit her lip. All the awkwardness was forgotten. She felt as if her heart was literally reaching out for Alex, straining against her ribcage.

Alex had stretched himself to his limit to keep going through all this mess. Maybe even before that. Maybe he'd been holding himself tight together ever since Becky had left him. She thought back to the first night she'd met him, how he'd had that undercurrent of power and intensity, how he'd seemed hyper-aware, edgy. It had been rather intoxicating. She hadn't guessed just what it must have cost him to stay strong for everyone else, ignoring his own needs.

For a while he'd been fuelled by adrenalin, doing what needed to be done because that was what Alex Dangerfield did. But the emergency was over now. They were supposed to be quietly getting on with their lives. The dullness in his eyes told her Alex's adrenalin had drained away. Unfortunately, she suspected they still had a bumpy road ahead of the three of them so, in some ways, the struggle had only just begun. Just as Alex had reached the end of himself.

Jennie put her glass down. Although Alex would never admit to being anything less than omnipotent, right at this moment her husband needed someone to share his load. Unfortunately for the poor guy, she was the only candidate, so he was just going to have to put up with whatever haphazard help she could offer.

She unfolded herself from her chair, crossed the room, took his glass from him and placed it on the low coffee table. Then she knelt next to him on the long leather sofa, looked into his eyes and ran her fingertips softly across his shoulders. He shivered at her touch and closed his eyes.

She might not have a great scientific brain, able to provide DNA results to soothe his ridged brow. She might not be Supernanny, ready to transform any kid from monster to angel with a sticker chart and a naughty step. Her only skills lay in guest lists, canapés and booking venues. And knowing how to help people have a great time, to feel good.

That much she could do for him.

Alex needed time out of his life, to feel something other than despair, to think about something other than the problems that consumed him. She had a sneaking suspicion that had been her attraction for him in the first place, so she might as well do her job. She could make him forget—at least until morning.

She shifted one leg so she was sitting across his lap facing him, a knee on either side of his thighs, and then she leaned forward and kissed him. Softly. Tenderly. Putting all her heart into it—the way she'd been aching to do ever since he'd turned up at Alice and Cameron's reception.

He met her eagerly, pulling her towards him, sliding his fingers under the hem of her blouse to feel her skin, and her breath hitched. Blindly, she reached for the top button of his shirt and fumbled with it.

Oh, yes. She was going to make Alex feel good. Very, very good.

Alex woke, as he usually did, well before dawn the next morning, and for a few blessed moments he felt totally relaxed, totally peaceful. Jennie was curled up against him, breathing softly. He kissed her bare shoulder gently enough not to wake her.

It shocked him how much he loved her. He'd never loved Becky this way.

As he lay there, slowly waking, these strange

thoughts flooding his head, the events of the previous day started to sharpen and come into focus. The cold dread he'd been trying to ignore returned and he closed his eyes, willing his pulse rate to flatten, willing himself back onto an even keel.

Jennie's arm twitched and she sighed gently, then burrowed closer to him. He twisted his head and looked at the alarm clock. Six-thirty. Not a time of day that Jennie habituated. Far from it. Much as he hated to leave her, his brain was whirring now and he feared he'd disturb her if he stayed much longer, so he gently eased himself out of bed and dressed quietly in the bathroom before padding downstairs.

He was sitting at the kitchen table with a cup of tea in front of him when Mollie appeared. She poked just her head round the door, her eyes wide and blinking, her mouth gathered into a tense pout. She was waiting to see what he'd do, what he'd say. He softened the grim line of his mouth into the beginnings of a smile, let the warmth shine out of his eyes. She walked slowly over to him and stood there looking very forlorn. The thumb on her right hand protruded from her tiny fist and, after a moment's hesitation, she stuck it in her mouth.

'You mustn't run off without asking a grown-up, okay?' he said, resisting the urge to reach for her and pull her close, just in case it would be too much for her.

She blinked again.

'Do you think you can do that?'

She frowned, deep lines appearing on her fore-head—much too deep for a three-year-old.

Jennie had told him of her conversation with Mollie as they'd lain wrapped around each other in the dark last night. A thought hit him. 'And perhaps we can go and visit Mummy's grave, take her some flowers and those lovely cards you've made her.' The light returned to Mollie's eyes and she gave him the slightest, sweetest smile. Before she started bugging him about the lack of chocolate cereal in the house and whether she could have boiled eggs and soldiers for breakfast, she leaned against him so their arms touched and pressed into him. Almost, *almost* lay her head on his shoulder. And then she was gone again.

Alex let out the breath he'd been holding. Maybe it was better she was holding back still. It made it easier for him not to get too attached. She was so sweet, so beautiful. If it turned out…

He flattened that feeling out, too, couldn't even think about it. Instead, his mind strayed to the case he was trying. Although it was complex, it was much more comfortable than thinking about Mollie. In a week or two they'd know for sure, and then he could breathe out and enjoy the little girl he was starting to lose his heart to.

Jennie woke to the smell of warm coffee. She stretched like a cat and opened her eyes to find Alex smiling at her. Boy, her husband was gorgeous when he smiled. And, after last night, she hoped he had a lot to smile about. A long sigh, mixed with a yawn escaped her lips.

Her hunch had been correct—it had been different between them. But *better* different. Not just heat and fire, although that had been there in abundance, but…*richer,* too.

'Good morning,' she said, injecting a smile into the remnants of her yawn.

Alex just placed a mug of coffee on the bedside table and leaned forward to kiss her. And kiss her again. And again. And… Well, the coffee had gone cold by the time she remembered it was there.

'I'll make you another one,' he said, putting his shirt back on and looking a little sheepish.

Jennie smiled. She didn't care about coffee. All she cared about was that somehow, last night, even after all the turmoil, she and Alex had found a way back to each other. They were no longer dancing around each other like boxers, keeping themselves beyond the other's reach if there was a hint they might inflict any further damage. This morning she was in the centre of his world again, right where she wanted to be.

CHAPTER TEN

JENNIE helped her stepmother clear the dishes while the rest of the family argued over the last piece of pavlova. Cameron was putting forward a very good case, but he didn't have Mollie's cute factor. Alice and Alex were cheering their respective loved ones on, and her father was relishing his role as judge and jury.

It had taken a few weeks before they'd been able to get them all together on a Sunday for a family lunch. Alice and Cameron had been on honeymoon and her parents had taken a short trip away to relax after all the wedding madness, and this was the first time both her father and Alice and Cameron had met her new family properly.

Jennie carefully put the pile of plates she'd been carrying down near the sink. 'That was an incredible lunch, Marion.' She smiled. 'Made me realise how much I've got to learn. I've only just mastered boiling eggs.'

Marion put down the large serving plate she'd been carrying. 'Are you sure you know what you're doing?'

Jennie nodded brightly. 'Boiling water, salt and then three minutes…hang on.' She frowned. 'Or is it four?'

'No,' Marion said. 'I meant with Alex and Mollie…'

The smile slid from Jennie's face. Of all people, she would have thought that Marion would be the one to understand, to support her.

Marion looked pained, but she clasped her hands in front of her and carried on talking. 'I just need to know…' she started, but then she shook her head and began again. 'You've dived into so many things without thinking…and I can't fault your enthusiasm, but this isn't some silly scrape you can sweet-talk your way out of when it's not fun any longer. This is for life.'

'I know that.' Jennie's hands felt all clammy and cold. She folded them into the crooks of her elbows and hugged herself tight. 'Don't you… Don't you think I can do this?'

Marion walked towards her, face full of compassion. 'I'm not saying that, but…' She glanced in the direction of the dining room. 'You haven't chosen an easy path. I look at that wonderful man and that darling girl and I see...' She gently gripped Jennie's upper arms, held her. 'Those two come with baggage. Lots of it. There's going to be heartache as well as joy ahead.'

The sinking feeling in Jennie's stomach overrode her instant mental denial at Marion's statement. She stared at the kitchen door. Mollie cheered in the other room and Cameron gave an overly theatrical groan. She knew who'd won her father over in the end and it made her smile, made the cold churning stop.

'I know what I've got myself into.' She looked into Marion's eyes. 'And I know it isn't going to be easy—it might even be my ultimate scrape...' She let out a dry laugh. 'But of all the scrapes I've ever got myself into, this is the one that's worth it. I love him, Marion. I love them both. I don't care whether it's sensible or not, whether it's going to be easy or not—I'm sticking with it.'

Marion drew her into a fragrant hug and Jennie realised she always associated her stepmother's perfume with peace and calm. 'Good girl,' Marion whispered. 'If you attack it with that attitude, you'll be fine in the end. And I'm here for you whenever you need me.'

Jennie hugged her back. 'Thank you,' she replied softly.

Alex stared at the large cardboard envelope the courier had delivered to his chambers. While there was a strong chance it contained legal documents, his gut told him otherwise. It was what he'd been holding out for. What he feared most.

The results of Mollie's DNA test.

He placed the envelope carefully on his desk, making sure it was square to the edges, and stared at it some more. It was bizarre. He was the man who never backed down from facing anything, who always honoured his commitments, yet he was awfully tempted to stuff it in a drawer and pretend it didn't exist.

He was concerned that Jennie had allowed herself to get too attached to Mollie. He'd tried to warn her, but she hadn't listened. She hadn't hesitated at the threshold of parenthood as he had; she'd done what she always did—thrown herself in at the deep end and worried about whether she could actually do it later.

She was going to be a wonderful mother.

Already was, he supposed. Okay, she didn't always follow the traditional approach, but it was clear that Mollie was beginning to adore her, too. What if the contents of this letter ripped all of that apart? It would break her heart.

Carefully and methodically, he packed his dark thoughts away in a place he'd built specially in the back of his head. But there was so much stored in there now the pressure was getting too much. Although Alex didn't consciously notice it, the darkness started to seep through the cracks, tainting everything with shadows until the few colours inside him were gradually swallowed up with shades of grey.

He picked up the envelope, suddenly feeling much better, much more...well, just not feeling the overwhelming sense of panic creeping up on him any more, not feeling much of anything, really. It was a relief, he realised, to have reached this point, to have finally come to terms with the chaos of the last month or two.

He inhaled and tore off the strip from the courier's envelope and a smaller white one dropped out. Before he could psych himself out of opening that one, too, he ripped it open, unfolded the single sheet and scanned down the printed page until he found what he was looking for.

Only a ninety-nine point nine per cent chance...

Of what? That he was or he wasn't?

He forced himself to focus and read the lines of print, not just the numbers, and then clutched the flimsy bit of paper to his chest. The samples matched. Mollie was his. He breathed out, reached for the phone and dialled Jennie's number.

The sofa was calling to him. He hadn't sat down and done nothing for weeks. Too many things had been going round his head, making him restless. He'd thought getting the DNA results last week would help, but his thoughts had only picked up speed.

He sank into the sofa and leaned his head against the back cushion, but he couldn't get himself comfy. Nothing felt right. He shifted his head and tried to create a dent for it. Eventually he found a position that wasn't perfect but worked.

Jennie was meeting Alice and that mad Coreen up in London later. A crisis meeting to discuss man trouble, or something like that. Alex shuddered. He was very happy to have been left out of the loop on that one.

He'd tried breathing in through his nose and out through his mouth. That was supposed to be relaxing, wasn't it? Unfortunately, he didn't get a chance to see whether it worked or not because he'd only managed four and half breaths when a high-pitched cry ruined his concentration.

He sprang off the sofa and pounded up the stairs just in time to see a half-dressed, half-made-up Jennie disappear into Mollie's room. He charged in after her, hitting the light switch as he did so. Jennie scooped Mollie into her arms and sat down on the bed with her.

It took Alex a couple of seconds to get his bearings. He still wasn't used to seeing a riot of pink and prettiness where the elegant guest room once had been. Jennie had managed miracles in a few short weeks. Unfortunately, he suspected it would take a lot more nodding at swatches and handing over his credit card before she was finished.

Jennie rocked Mollie gently, cradling her against her shoulder. 'What's up, Princess?' she murmured into Mollie's hair. The squealing had stopped, but Mollie's eyes were wet and pink and she heaved in a breath that shuddered through every part of her tiny frame before putting her lips to Jennie's ear.

Alex stepped forward, not sure what to do. Jennie swivelled round so he could see her face, still holding Mollie close, and mouthed the word *monsters* at him.

'Where are they?' she asked Mollie.

Alex frowned. Surely she should be dispelling the silly idea of monsters, not encouraging it.

'In the cupboard,' Mollie whispered and pointed emphatically at the built-in cupboard on one side of the chimney breast whilst clutching Jennie even harder.

Jennie peeled Mollie off her shoulder and put her on her lap. 'Well, I think we have a big, strong man somewhere in the house to protect us. I'm sure he'll scare them all away if we ask him to.' She looked deliberately in Alex's direction, then tapped her cheek with a fingertip. 'Hmm. Now where do you suppose he could be?'

Mollie started to giggle softly and pointed at Alex.

'Ah, yes,' Jennie said very seriously. 'I knew I'd left him somewhere.'

Mollie giggled harder.

'Now, why don't you give Daddy that nice new torch I bought you, and he can check in the cupboard for us.'

Still gripping on to Jennie, Mollie leaned over and retrieved a chunky, colourful toy torch from under the corner of her duvet. It never ceased to surprise Alex just how much junk Mollie insisted on having in her bed. There were so many soft toys he was surprised she could find a flat space to sleep on.

Jennie passed the torch to Alex and gave him an encouraging look. He shrugged, turned the large red button on the torch and marched over to the half-open cupboard door.

'I think he'd scare *me* away if he came after me like that,' Jennie whispered behind his back.

'Do it, Daddy!' Mollie said, bouncing on Jennie's lap. 'Scare the monsters 'way!'

This was ridiculous. Still, he made a show of opening the cupboard door and shining the torch around. 'See? No monsters in there.' He looked over his shoulder at Jennie and Mollie. 'Come and have a look.'

Mollie shook her head and dived under the covers.

'Don't be silly,' he said, walking back over to

the bed and flipping the duvet aside. 'Come and look.'

Mollie just squealed and shoved the pillow over her head.

'There are no monsters,' Alex said, aware that if he'd had a playful edge to his voice to start off with, he'd definitely lost it now. 'Monsters aren't real.'

A muffled voice came from under the pillow. He looked at Jennie, hoping she'd translate. She gave him an exasperated look and said, 'They're invisible monsters, apparently. And just because they've disappeared now, doesn't mean they won't come back again.'

He handed her the torch. 'If you're such an expert, perhaps you'd like to deal with them?'

Jennie stood up and put her hands on her hips. 'Since it seems our dashing hero has turned into a grumpy old troll,' she said, talking to Mollie but looking pointedly at him, 'I've got something in my room that will help us deal with those monsters.'

She left Alex standing there and left the room, only to return a few moments later, holding something in her hand. She sat down on the bed and prised the pillow from Mollie's grip.

'Look.' Jennie dangled a pink plastic jewel on a pink ribbon in front of Mollie, who sat up and grabbed it instantly. 'Now,' said Jennie, sliding Mollie onto her lap, 'you have to promise me you'll look after this because it's very special.'

Mollie's eyes grew large and round and she nodded at least six times.

'This is a magic pendant that is very good at scaring away monsters. Can you hand me Teddy?' Mollie stuck an arm under the duvet and produced her favourite bear. 'It's not good for little girls to wear necklaces while they're sleeping, so I'm going to let Teddy look after this.' She fastened the pendant around Teddy's neck and gave him to Mollie, who squeezed him tight. 'But as long as you're cuddling Teddy it won't matter even if the monsters do come back, because that jewel means they can't hurt you.' She looked upwards and smiled, as if she'd just remembered something. 'In fact, when Teddy's got the necklace on, if you even *look* at a monster it's going to shrivel up and turn to dust. So, if you think they've come back, shine your torch on them and say the magic words...'

She turned to look at Alex and raised her eyes. What? He was supposed to know what the magic words were? If he knew any magic words, he'd have used them on himself to stop himself turning invisible, because that was what seemed to be happening to him.

Look at Jennie, making monster-catching fun. It should be him doing that. He should be the one protecting his daughter. All he'd had to do was join in, shine a torch around a cupboard and say a few nonsense words, and he hadn't even been able to manage that. He finally had the family he'd always dreamed of, but, ironically, he didn't seem to be part of it. He couldn't even keep his daughter safe from *imaginary* monsters, for goodness' sake!

'Well, now we've sorted all of that out, I've got to finish getting ready,' Jennie said brightly. She kissed Mollie on the forehead and disappeared back to their bedroom. Mollie looked at him.

'What?' he said. Was there something else he was expected to do? Dance a little jig? Stand on his head?

'Jennie's busy,' Mollie said and held a book up.

Alex took it from her and sat on the far end of the bed. 'I'm not sure I can do the voices as well as Jennie, but I'll give it a go.'

Mollie smiled sweetly at him and, instead of tucking herself in down the other end of the bed as he'd expected, she climbed into his lap, settled herself there and tapped the book with a finger. *'Read.'*

For a moment Alex didn't move. It felt so alien, having a little warm body curled up against his. Mollie tapped the book impatiently once more and he opened it and started to read. It wasn't long before his mind was elsewhere, only involving itself in the story enough to keep the words falling out of his mouth.

This was what he'd been waiting for.

All he'd wanted since he'd known Mollie might be his was to have her in his arms, to share the easy affection he'd seen other fathers share with their kids. It was almost as if he'd known that, when this moment came, the last piece of his disassembled life would clunk back into place and the world would start spinning again.

He held his breath. He waited. But nothing happened.

He felt the warmth of her skin through her pyjamas, did his best to mould into her, but he felt stiff and cold. What was wrong with him?

* * *

Coreen winked at Jennie and Alice as the barman placed identical gaudy-looking cocktails in front of them.

'What on earth is *that?*' Jennie said, lifting the umbrella out and looking warily at it.

Coreen sipped hers through the glittery straw, not pausing until she'd run out of oxygen. 'It's called a Runaway Train. House speciality. Just the thing when the man in your life is driving you crazy.'

Jennie took a tentative sip. *Wow!*

And then she took another.

'*Is* there a man in your life?' she said. 'I thought you were between lovelorn swains.'

Coreen grimaced. 'That, my darling, is the problem.'

Jennie just laughed. The idea of Coreen not being able to command male attention was just plain ridiculous. With her wild vintage look, her glossy red lips, her eye-popping curves, well, you could sum her up in one word—naughty. And, last time she checked, the male of the species liked *naughty*.

'There's this guy…' Coreen's shoulders sagged forward and she took another sip of her cocktail.

When she'd finished, she looked at Jennie. 'How did you get Alex to propose so fast?'

Jennie had been getting ready to quip about man-eating Coreen finding a man who didn't want to nibble her back, but Coreen's question took her by surprise. *Whoa.* For her friend to be thinking proposals, this guy must be something else.

'I didn't *get* him to do it,' she replied. 'He came up with the idea all by himself.'

Coreen nodded encouragingly. 'Okay…so how did you get him to come up with the idea all by himself?'

Jennie laughed again and cooled herself with a sip of Runaway Train. Coreen had spent so much of her life winding men around her little finger that she'd forgotten they often had a will of their own.

Alice's eyes opened wide. 'You've got it bad!'

Coreen sighed. 'He thinks I'm a minor annoyance—if he thinks of me at all.'

'Ouch,' Jennie said.

Coreen picked the slice of pineapple off the rim of her glass and sucked it. 'So how *did* Alex propose, anyway? You kept it all such a secret we never found out. Was it wildly romantic?'

'Yes…and no. It wasn't flowers and champagne and fireworks—'

Coreen bounced on her chair. 'Ooh! I love fireworks. If I ever get a proposal, I want there to be fireworks!'

Jennie shrugged. 'Sorry. None of that stuff. But it *was* romantic.'

'Cameron's proposal was *very* romantic,' Alice sighed. 'It was just before Christmas—'

'Yes, yes,' Coreen said with a dismissive wave of her hand. 'We've all heard the story a million times before! What I want is to hear about *Jennie's* proposal.'

Alice narrowed her eyes at Coreen, even as an indulgent smile played on her lips. She got her revenge, though. Coreen leaned forward, her elbows on the bar and rested her chin on her knuckles. While she wasn't looking, Alice swapped her mostly empty cocktail glass for Coreen's almost-full one.

Jennie was about to laugh, but Coreen's expectant stare stopped her.

How did she explain it to Coreen without it seeming ordinary and run-of-the-mill? Because Alex's proposal hadn't felt that way at all. They'd both been working hard, hadn't seen each other for almost a week, and she'd come to meet him at King's Cross station as he'd returned from working on a case in Manchester. He hadn't known she was coming so she'd had to resort to scanning the crowd and, as rush hour had got underway, the concourse had got busier and busier and she'd started to panic she'd missed him altogether.

She told Coreen and Alice all of this.

'It's silly, really,' she added, blushing slightly. 'I couldn't see him anywhere...' She paused and pulled the tissue-wrapped memory from its careful storing place. She smiled dreamily, and the bar, the cocktail, all drifted away.

'And suddenly there he was—running towards me...'

Just thinking about it made her heart turn over. She'd sensed something moving fast in her peripheral vision and had turned around, and he'd been running towards her, not even looking at the commuters milling around waiting for their train to show up on the departures board. He'd just dodged them on instinct, never taking his eyes from her.

'It was the way he was looking at me,' she said. 'As if he couldn't see anything else. As if he didn't *want* to see anything else.'

Coreen clasped her hands together and sighed. 'See? That's what I'm talking about!'

Alice took a slurp of her drink. 'What happened next?'

Jennie's lips tingled. 'He kissed me.' Alex had kissed her until she'd felt giddy and alive and totally, totally lost in him. 'He was laughing...' She was almost whispering now. 'Even as he kissed me, he was laughing, and then he just said, "Let's do it" and I didn't even have to ask what he meant. I knew. I don't know how, but I knew.'

Coreen's eyebrows arched high and she stopped looking wistful. 'He didn't even say the words?'

Jennie shook her head, knowing that Coreen wasn't quite getting it, but it didn't matter. *She* got it. Who needed words when you could hear someone's heart?

And Alex's was such a good heart—strong, courageous, noble.

The image of him laughing returned, and it bothered her.

When had she last seen Alex laugh like that? When had she last seen him laugh at all? The Alex she lived with now was withdrawn and silent. If his heart was saying anything nowadays, she was deaf to it.

She hoped he'd slowly come out of it. She'd told herself he'd just needed time to recover from the shocks life had landed on him thick and fast but, stopped short by the memory of Alex's face that day, she couldn't ignore the truth any longer. Something was wrong between them.

Alice's voice broke though her thoughts. 'It's rather wonderful, isn't it?'

Jennie made a forgettable comment about the cocktail and Alice elbowed her in the ribs. 'Not the drink, you dafty! *Marriage!* I feel as if I'm in a perpetual state of bliss, don't you?'

'Yes.'

That was the answer Jennie was supposed to give but, as she and the girls chatted, her mind began to dissect her answer. She *was* happy with Alex. Wouldn't ever want to be with someone else, but…how did she put this? If she had to measure her level of happiness against Alice's *perpetual bliss,* she realised she wasn't hitting the mark.

On paper, everything should be perfect now between them: she was bonding with Mollie, and she and Alex had put the blip of their early marriage behind them. They had, hadn't they? Okay, Alex was working hard, as usual, but Cameron put in long hours, too, and Alice was still floating on a pink satin-lined cloud. Party-girl Jennie would have found that attitude slightly nauseating, but wife-and-mother Jennie was slightly…just a little bit…jealous. Where was her cloud of newly-wed happiness? Had they got past that stage already? It hardly seemed fair!

Coreen was right about the cocktail. A sense of clarity came over Jennie as she sipped it slowly. She listened with one ear as Coreen plotted how to get Mr Unimpressed to notice her and mulled over the problem of Alex.

Hadn't she struggled with the idea that maybe there had only been enough fuel in their relationship for a whirlwind affair? But she'd tucked that thought into the back of her mind, ignored it. Alex wasn't a playboy, for goodness' sake! And he'd had a long marriage with Becky—probably would still be with her, but for Becky's spectacular departure. So there was nothing wrong with the man she'd chosen.

She'd been sipping her Runaway Train through its straw, and she let it slide from her mouth.

What if Alex wasn't the problem? Perhaps it

was *her?* After all, she'd hardly ever had a long-term *anything.* Love had always come to her in fits and spurts. It wasn't a constant thing. There were seasons in every relationship—hot and cold, up and down. People came in and out of focus during the course of a person's life. That would explain boyfriends who had seemed fun for a while then lost their sparkle. Sometimes people faded away altogether—like her mother—or were a foggy presence in the background, like her father.

But she'd thought that when she got married it wouldn't be like that, that everything would finally be fixed. A sudden dryness at the back of her eyes made her blink. She didn't want Alex to fade away!

She'd also thought that when she found the right man she'd be able to retire from being the star of the show, the life and soul of the party. Because all that had just been an attempt to delay the inevitable—the moment when it was time for her to fade into the background, the moment when people looked away.

And she'd given up her attention-seeking ways when she'd met Alex because he'd *looked.* Really looked. Past the glitter and giggles. And he'd kept on looking. She'd said yes to his unspoken proposal because she'd thought she wouldn't need all the razzle dazzle to stop him looking away.

Coreen was still talking, and Jennie realised she really wasn't being a good friend. She tuned back in and listened properly.

'I've even tried going out with other men!' Coreen wailed.

'To make him jealous?' Alice said, shocked.

'No...' Coreen frowned. 'I've done that before. It's a terrible idea. I was just trying to distract myself, forget about him.'

Just trying to distract myself.

Jennie thought about Coreen's words constantly on the train home and in the taxi from the station.

Hadn't she used that word in reference to herself where Alex was concerned? A distraction. That was where the heart of it lay. Distractions were, by their very nature, temporary things. Perhaps her effectiveness had worn off now, maybe because Becky's death had finally brought him closure. Maybe he didn't need her in that way any more. Her insides started to ache.

The more she thought about it, the more she realised that Alex hadn't stopped distracting himself. He was still using that as his coping mechanism, the same way he always had. He was working hard—too hard—and she had the feeling it was partly by choice. This time *she* was the thing he was running away from.

She wanted to cry, really wanted to cry. But she clamped her jaw shut and blinked furiously. She hadn't promised Alex she'd be his *temporary distraction*. She'd promised him for ever. And that was what he was going to get.

Making people sit up and pay attention was her one true gift in life.

Not enough of a distraction for Alex Dangerfield? Well, she'd see about that.

One of Jennie's mad inspirations gripped her as she closed the front door behind her and hung up her coat. She didn't stop there; she kept going, unbuttoning her blouse and skirt, shimmying out of them and hanging them on a spare hook. The heels she kept on.

She could hear the muffled voice of a news-caster drifting from the living room as she walked to the open door. The television was on. Only the television, its flickering light making everything seem unreal and jerky. Alex was sitting on the sofa, totally absorbed in the football scores.

Not for long.

Jennie slid a hand up the door frame and draped herself fetchingly against it. Alex must have heard her breathy sigh because his head turned, almost automatically. And then his eyes widened. If she'd calculated it right, he was only three seconds away from drooling.

She walked towards him, seeing the fire ignite in his eyes, watching it sizzle brighter the closer she got.

She smiled and stopped in front of him.

She had his attention now. Oh, yes.

CHAPTER ELEVEN

LATE one night, with Alex dozing beside her, Jennie rolled onto her back, tucked her hands behind her head and stared at the ceiling.

Her plan had backfired. Or worked too well. She wasn't sure which.

Saucy lingerie and lots of *quality time* with Alex over the last few weeks hadn't solved anything. Yes, he was there in the moment with her when they made love, but it was the *only* time it happened. It hadn't bled into the rest of their lives.

To be honest, she wasn't sure she could take much more of this.

At least her relationship with Mollie was going from strength to strength. Jennie smiled at the ceiling. She'd never imagined being with a child that wasn't hers could bring such joy.

More than could be said for Mollie's father.

Being there in bed, great as it was, just wasn't

enough. She wanted more. She wanted all the things he'd promised—his heart, his soul, for eternity. She *needed* more. And you know what? She *deserved* more. She'd hung her 'pampered princess' crown up, never to be used again, that day she'd sat in the church and had chosen Alex. She'd finally grown up. She was trying very hard to be the sort of woman he needed. Why couldn't he see that? Why was she still invisible?

He always had a good sense of what time it was. Even before he opened his eyes, Alex knew it was later than he normally rose. A stab of panic hit him. He was late. There were things he needed to be doing, places he needed to be going. But before his brain could relay the signal to his muscles to contract then propel him out of bed it supplied another fact: it was Sunday.

That didn't change much. He still felt as if dogs were snapping at his heels, that he had to keep moving or something terrible would happen. And yet...

He could feel Jennie's warmth beside him, even though they weren't quite touching. Last night had been incredible. Maybe nothing dire would happen if he stayed in bed a few moments longer.

His warm and sexy wife was lying right next to him, and being with her was the only time the hounds were silenced, that he felt *right*.

He slid closer to her, ran his hand up a bare thigh. She felt so soft. It felt so good to touch her. He became totally absorbed in the friction between his fingertips and her leg, the curve he was following.

Jennie grunted and slapped his hand away.

He smiled. By no stretch of the imagination could his wife be described as a 'morning person'. But she might just change her mind, given the right incentive. He carried on where he'd left off.

She growled and turned over and away from him, and her mutter was muffled by half a pillow. 'Cut it out, Alex!'

He shuffled over again and kissed the shoulder that was sticking out of the duvet. Jennie tensed, then sprang out of bed. 'Alex! Take a hint, will you!'

She picked up her robe and shoved her arms into it. He didn't tell her she had it on inside out. It wouldn't go down well. He had a hunch something was up.

Who said men couldn't be intuitive and sensitive?

He propped himself up on one elbow. 'What's wrong?'

Jennie's fingers shook as she tied the sash of her robe into a ruthless knot. 'I can't live off your crumbs any more, Alex,' she half-whispered, glancing briefly in the direction of Mollie's bedroom.

Huh? What crumbs?

Alex blinked. 'Live like what?' he said slowly, refusing to look inside himself and find the answer to that question. Jennie gave him a look that only a disgruntled wife could give and only a thick-headed husband would ignore.

'I love you,' she said, her voice breaking slightly. 'But you won't let me in. You won't *let* me love you… I feel like our relationship is dying.' She paused and blinked slowly before looking across at him again. 'Do you love me, Alex, really? Or am I just a commitment you feel you have to honour?'

He obviously took too long in answering that one because she re-tied her sash even tighter and stomped from the room.

He flopped back down on the bed and stared at nothing, a horrible sense of déjà vu crawling over him. This was how it had started with

Becky. Incomprehensible outbursts. Cryptic ac-
cusations. His stomach clenched. Even though
he knew Jennie was much stronger than Becky,
much more resilient, he couldn't ignore the dread-
ful voice whispering in his ear.

*It's starting all over again. You'll lose her.
You'll lose everything.*

Alex sat up ramrod straight, his hands braced
against the mattress, then practically vaulted out
of bed. There was something vital he'd forgotten
to research for the case he was trying next week,
something that might just be key for the prosecution of a nasty thug.

He dressed mechanically, his mind already
having travelled ahead of him to his study downstairs. He didn't feel the carpet beneath his feet,
didn't know how many buttons he'd done up or
even what he'd put on. Mentally, he was running his fingers along his bookshelves, selecting
tomes, flicking to indexes and collecting facts.
Inside his head, everything was uncomplicated,
hard facts in black and white, not wispy phantom-
like emotions that couldn't be grasped let alone
comprehended. He liked the black and white.

And grey. Don't forget the grey.

* * *

'Daddy?'

Alex looked up from the paperwork strewn all over his study desk. 'Yes, Mollie?'

She sidled into the room, looking freshly bathed and as cute as could be in her pink pyjamas, and held up a colourful book about a ballet-dancing mouse. He put his pen down and looked at her hopeful smile. 'Not now, okay? Daddy's busy.'

The smile stayed, but the hopeful quality drained away. 'Please, Daddy?'

He didn't want to send her away, didn't want to pretend the stuff covering his desk was more important, but the thought of snuggling up on the sofa with her filled him with terror. Every time he tried to connect with Mollie the same fog descended upon him, deadening everything until he was blind and useless. He couldn't do it any more. He couldn't sit curled up with her, knowing he should be feeling things he didn't, knowing he was letting her down.

She was too small to understand at the moment, but eventually she would sense the deadness, too, and he wanted to spare her that. It would be easier for her to think that he had no choice than to realise her father didn't know how to love her.

Perhaps this was what happened in situations like theirs—when parent and child had been disconnected before birth and too much time had passed until they were reunited again. People always said bonding was important, that new mums needed to spend lots of time with their newborns after the birth. Perhaps there was a time limit. Maybe, if bonding didn't occur within a certain time, it never would. The connection was severed.

But then why did Mollie not feel the same way?

It was all too confusing. And, until he could find a way to make it all work properly, it was better if he kept his distance—to protect Mollie, of course.

'Not tonight,' he said to his daughter, knowing he was about to lie. 'Maybe tomorrow.'

She nodded sadly and left the room, leaving the door ajar. He got up to close it, to shut the guilt outside and keep it there, but before he reached it Jennie stepped inside.

'She was really looking forward to reading that book with you,' she said.

He backed away and sat down at his desk, made his face conform to something resembling disappointment. He used his hands to answer for him, indicating the papers hiding the surface of his desk.

Jennie looked as if she was going to say something but then changed her mind. Instead, she headed for the door. Alex breathed a silent sigh of relief. He didn't want to talk to Jennie about this; he felt awful enough as it was. And he feared whatever disease he had was spreading. Sometimes he looked at his amazing wife and he didn't feel anything then, either.

A warm thought invaded his mind. Except, of course, after Mollie had gone to bed, and he and Jennie got to spend some adult time together. Those times in bed with Jennie were islands of sensation that he was becoming more and more dependent on. At least when he was with her in bed he knew he hadn't turned to stone.

'Are you going to be much longer?' Jennie asked, eyeing his desk suspiciously.

He nodded, but then he got up, walked over to her and snatched a sweet, drugging kiss. 'I'll be finished before bedtime, I promise,' he said, a hint of wickedness creeping into his tone.

Weeks ago, Jennie would have laughed her sweet, husky laugh and persuaded him she was ready to go upstairs right now, but this evening she just nodded and left the room, closing the door firmly behind her.

Alex wandered back to his desk and sat down. He put his elbows on the desk, creasing a page of notes, and rested his chin on his fists. He had the horrible feeling things might be even worse than he'd thought.

What if this thing he had—this anaesthesia—was catching? He didn't want to believe that his vibrant, beautiful wife might fade away as he had, all the light seeping out of her, but he couldn't ignore that things were different between them. Something must have happened, and he tried hard not to think that it was his fault, that he had infected her, too.

Almost another week went by before Jennie finally cracked. It was Saturday, and Alex was at his chambers—again. Instead of trying to talk to her about what was going on between them, he'd decided to make himself so busy that he always had a good excuse to stay late at work or disappear into his study when she looked as if she might be about to get deeper than *How was your day?* or *What do you want for dinner?*

She knew he was struggling, and she was trying to be patient, but it had been a month since the DNA test results had come back and Alex was as distant and as…absent…as ever. She was at the end of her rope. So she was going to pack a bag and when Alex got home this evening she would tell him she was going to spend a few days in her flat up in town. She needed to give herself some breathing space, give herself time to think. Give Alex some time to think, too. Maybe he'd work out if he really wanted her around or not. When he'd decided, he could come and get her.

She listlessly pulled a small case out of the cupboard, heaved it onto the bed and started opening drawers and piling stuff into it. Glittery stuff, sparkly stuff. Party stuff. While she was in London she was going to go out and have a good time. At least, that was what she told herself as she haphazardly filled the case. Better than admitting she was just going to sit in her old flat and cry.

The case was three-quarters full when she heard a noise behind her. She whipped around, clutching a shoe to her chest. Mollie had been playing in her room, but now she was standing in the doorway, her face a picture of horror.

'Wh-what you…doing?' Her lips trembled and her face was pale.

Jennie's mouth moved. She didn't want to tell Mollie. Tears started to run down the little girl's face, and then she ran to Jennie, threw her arms round her middle and squeezed her breathlessly tight.

'Don't go!' she sobbed into Jennie's chest. 'Don't want you to.'

She was practically hysterical now. Jennie flung the shoe away and hugged Mollie just as hard back, then bent over and kissed Mollie's head. 'Shh. Don't cry.' But it was no use. Mollie was in full flood, didn't seem to be able to control herself. Jennie's throat felt swollen and tight when she spoke. 'Shh. I'm not going anywhere, darling. I promise I'm going to stay right here with you.'

Mollie gulped and pulled away just enough to lean back and look up at her. 'B-but you…' her face crumpled '…p-packing.'

Pain hit Jennie square in the chest. Mollie's pain, not her own. This poor little girl had had too many empty spaces where love should have been in her life. Jennie didn't have the heart to add herself to that number. Alex might not need her any more, but Mollie did. She wasn't going to let her own selfish little tantrum upset the fragile equilibrium they'd established.

She tried to peel herself away from Mollie, but Mollie just starting screaming and clutching at her even harder. The noise went straight through Jennie's ears and into her heart. She gave in, hugged Mollie, kissed Mollie, until she calmed down. When she relaxed her grip a little, Jennie lifted Mollie's face so they were looking at each other. *Trust me,* she told Mollie with her eyes, then she moved away slowly.

The little girl looked as if she was about to panic again, so Jennie acted quickly. She picked up her case, dumped the entire contents on the floor and threw the case back inside the cupboard. When she'd finished, she ran to Mollie. They clung to each other so hard that standing became difficult, so they crumpled onto the floor rather than let go, and Mollie ended up sitting across Jennie's folded legs.

Jennie held her tight and stroked her hair, something she remembered her own mother doing when she'd been a little girl.

She felt this…this…fierce sense of protectiveness towards her stepdaughter, and it scared her.

She felt as if she would rip anybody limb from limb who wanted to hurt her, and she wished she could just open her heart and pour the contents inside Mollie, so desperate was she for her to know how much she was loved. Jennie's eyes were sticky and her nose threatened to drip. She hadn't even been aware she'd been crying, too.

Eventually the crushing desperation lifted and they relaxed against each other, just breathing.

Was this what mothers felt like? It was nothing like the warm, cosy feeling she'd thought it would be. It was overpowering. Overwhelming. And very, very scary to love something this much. The sort of thing you might be tempted to run away from if it all got too intense.

'I'm sorry,' she whispered into Mollie's hair. 'I didn't meant to scare you. I was just…'

Running away from her problems.

Was that what she'd been about to do? She searched deep inside herself and realised that to be partly true. But she hadn't been in the same kind of frenzy she'd been when she'd packed in Paris. This time it hadn't been about wanting to be found, because she wasn't even sure Alex would come. That kind of running away had been about hope. This time she'd been packing because she'd thought there was none.

She kissed the top of Mollie's head again.

Well, she was staying, not leaving this time. Which meant she was in uncharted territory. And she was going to have to find a way to get through to Alex, because she'd been right about one thing: she couldn't live like this any longer. She was going to have to fight for Alex. First things first, though.

She looked down at Mollie. 'How about a picnic for lunch?' The day had turned warm and sunny and it would be lovely to sit out in the garden and relax.

Mollie grinned at her. Her eyes were still pink and her face was still blotchy—hardcore crying really didn't suit her pale colouring. 'Can we have Marmite sandwiches?'

'Absolutely.'

'In the tree house?'

Jennie thought for a second, and then she shrugged. 'Why not? It'll be fun.'

Mollie cheered softly and clambered from her lap. 'I'm going to tell Teddy!' She ran across the room, but stopped at the threshold to look back. 'Can Teddy have Marmite sandwiches, too?'

Before Jennie could agree, Mollie spoke from behind her hand in a loud stage whisper. 'Teddy can't really eat sandwiches. I have to help him.'

Jennie laughed. 'Teddy can have a small one.'

Mollie ran off to break the good news to Teddy.

Jennie didn't get up off the floor straight away. Instead, she hugged her knees to herself and rested her chin on them. She'd tried to fight for Alex already, she realised, but she'd used all the wrong weapons—the tried and trusted methods of her childhood. All that had done was leave a bitter taste in her mouth. It wasn't about getting what *she* wanted any more, anyway. She needed to find a new way to fight for her marriage.

This was what people did when they'd made vows to each other—when one was weak and hurting, the other stepped in and was strong *for* them. And it felt good to be strong for Alex. Nobody had ever needed her to be the strong one before. She'd always been the one who ran to other people, begging them to bail her out of her latest mess.

Not fair, the child inside her screamed. Why should *you* have to be the one to make the first move, make all the sacrifices?

Because someone had to. Someone had to stop the slow drifting. Someone had to close the gap before it was too late. And, after watching Alex for the last few weeks, she realised he just wasn't capable.

CHAPTER TWELVE

ALEX jerked awake. Another convoluted dream where he was chasing something. Or was it running from something? Or searching. Endlessly searching. The details were already muddled and fuzzy, retreating into his subconscious. He lay there in the dark, his breathing shallow.

He'd been having dreams like this for weeks now. Funnily enough, ever since that night when Mollie had found monsters in her cupboard. They hadn't returned to bother her, and he had a hunch he knew why—they'd turned their attention to him.

Jennie was sleeping beside him. He could curl into her, leach some comfort from her warm, sleeping form, but he didn't want to wake her. Not for any noble reason, merely because she'd want to know what was wrong, and he didn't think he could handle any more of her kindness.

He knew he was failing her as a husband, but

he couldn't seem to do a damned thing about it. Maybe his brother Chris had been right. Maybe he *had* rushed headlong into another marriage before he'd been ready for it, but he didn't want to think about that. He was scared enough of what he'd done to Jennie, what he was putting her through every day. He didn't need any more guilt weighing him down.

He backed a little bit closer to her. She seemed a different person from the woman he'd met in Edward's back garden. That was scaring him, too, not because he felt as if he didn't know her any more, but because she was blooming on the outside into the wonderful woman he'd always known she was on the inside, whereas he was shrivelling into a dry husk.

Jennie rolled over and he held his breath, and then a long-fingered hand brushed his arm. His heart sank.

'Hey,' she said, her voice warm with sleep.

He couldn't reply. He'd betray himself. So he just found her hand with his and squeezed it.

'Dreaming again?'

How did she know? He hadn't told her about his dreams. But she seemed to guess a lot of things about him these days. He didn't want her seeing inside him like this. It was dark in there—and empty. It must be. Because nothing light or happy ever came out of him. All the patience and joy and life Jennie gave him just got sucked in and were never seen again.

He just grunted, hoping the non-committal noise would be enough.

She sighed, and for a while he thought she was drifting back to sleep, but then the mattress shifted as she repositioned herself. 'You're not happy,' she said. It wasn't a question.

He felt sick. He didn't want to agree with her, didn't want to hurt her that way. She shuffled closer, spooned in behind him, stroked his arm and then hugged him tight, her chin resting in the crook of his shoulder.

'I wanted to run from this, ignore this—anything but face it,' she said. 'But we can't go on like this. You've got to let it all out, Alex. It's eating you alive.'

He closed his eyes and fervently wished he could rewind time to back before their wedding, when everything had been fresh and uncompli- cated. But then he wouldn't know her the way he knew her now, and he loved her so much more for giving him her strength and patience, her devotion—even when he didn't deserve it.

'I haven't given up on you, Alex, but I need to know if you've given up on me.'

He opened his mouth, but she shushed him.

'Let me finish... I know this is hard for you, but I need to tell you that I almost packed a bag and left you a couple of weeks ago.'

The cold dread he'd been trying to outrun suddenly turned into a brick wall. He smacked straight into it. She'd almost left him? And he hadn't even guessed. Hadn't seen it coming. He was failing another wife.

She waited for him while he processed this information and now she took his silence as he'd meant it—an invitation to continue.

'We all have things we need to face,' she whispered. 'I decided it was time to stop running. Time to stick with what I'd started, no matter how hard it got.'

He should have felt grateful at that, should have felt his stomach thaw out, but it just got harder and colder and tighter. He blinked and stared at the wall. 'I always thought you were a miracle of some kind, Jennie Hunter.'

She didn't say anything for a few seconds. She

was wrapped around him and he felt her muscles lose that heavy, fluid feel. When she spoke again her voice was thick. 'Dangerfield. My name is Jennie *Dangerfield.*'

And then she pulled away from him. He felt and heard her hit the mattress, and guessed she'd rolled onto her back.

Well done, Alex.

Minutes limped by and then Jennie said, 'Chris phoned and asked you to go climbing in Scotland, didn't he? Some annual trip you do. I think you should go.'

Why was she bringing this up? He'd done the right thing about that.

'I told him I wasn't going,' he said, and heard the irritation in his own voice. 'Work's busy. I hardly get to spend any time with you and Mollie as it is.'

Jennie let out a sad, resigned breath. 'Even when you're here, you're not really here. And the more time you spend…*ghost walking* around this house, the worse it gets. We need you, Alex—me and Mollie. We need you to be here with us, not just in body, but *here*…'

She reached out and placed a warm palm on his chest, left it there for a few seconds, then drew it away again. 'You once told me I was like a roller coaster ride,' she said, her voice bare. 'I was flattered. But I'm not sure you want a roller coaster. I think you like the flat of the motorway better—even speed, no lumps and bumps, inter-changeable scenery...'

'That's not true! I—'

'We had a concentrated high at the beginning of our relationship, but it can't always be like that, you realise that, don't you? There are going to be low patches, tough times. We can't shut our eyes and pretend they don't exist.'

He folded his arms across his chest. 'I'm not shutting my eyes against anything.'

Jennie seemed to know he was kidding himself because she carried on. 'You can't have the highs without the lows, you know. And if you want to iron it all flat and go without both...well...that's not living. It's existing. You need to decide what you want,' she added, her voice cooler now. 'The motorway or the roller coaster. And time away might help you do that.'

Alex rolled onto his back. 'I know what I want.'

He'd always known what he wanted; he'd always had the whole of his life planned out, right from the age of fifteen, when he'd decided he was going to study law to help people, to protect people. But he realised now that Jennie had never really been part of his plans. She'd been an impulse, a wonderful, maddening, life-affirming impulse. What did that mean?

'I'll tell you what I want,' she said, her voice heavy with sadness. 'Having Mollie and I under the same roof as you isn't the same as being a family, and I want to have the future we dreamed about, even if it looks a little different now we're here.'

He couldn't take it any more. He rolled over to face her. 'I want that, too,' he found himself saying. 'But I don't know how.' And as the words left his mouth he felt raw and open, all his weakness on display.

She reached out and touched his cheek. Even when he was breaking her heart she was still generous to him.

'If you want to, you'll find a way.' It wasn't an accusation, but a fact, stated with love and tinged with fear. 'But...' her voice dried '...if it's not happening, you have to ask yourself if this is what you *really* want. Am *I* what you really want, or was I just the best way to forget your problems, another way to distance yourself from your feelings when everything got too much?'

Shame washed over him. It was true what she'd said—partly. He'd used her, and he was an utter heel for doing it, but he loved her, too. At least, he had. He wasn't sure of what he felt about anything any more. He just hoped he could untangle all of this and still find that love when he was free of it, that it wouldn't disappear along with the knots.

He pulled her to him, kissed her cheek and tasted her quiet tears.

'I'll go,' he said. 'To Scotland.'

She softened just a little in his arms, but he was terrified as he lay there very still, holding her. Terrified he'd find he was wrong. That he didn't want her after all. How could he tell when he was this numb?

The air up here was so clean, so pure. Alex stopped walking up the rock-strewn ridge and turned to look around him. As far as the eye could see, there was nothing man-made. He couldn't even spot a crofter's cottage or a road. No power lines. Not even an aeroplane in the sky. Just craggy mountains, mists of purple heather, rough grass and swathes of bracken. And the clear, bright sky.

He could almost imagine he was the only living soul on the planet. No other people meant no relationships to mess up. He was sure this soaring solitary feeling would eventually ground itself and become crushing loneliness, but at the moment he felt wonderfully free.

'Hey, slowcoach! If you don't get a move on, we won't reach the summit by lunchtime and I'm hungry.'

Alex turned his head and found his brother grinning at him.

Well, he was *almost* the last soul on the planet.

Thankfully, Chris, while good-natured and cheerful, knew when to leave Alex to his own thoughts. He didn't bombard him with chatter as they climbed. He didn't sing stupid songs at the top of his voice. Alex loved his brother.

To ensure Chris's continuing silence, he stopped admiring the view and started putting one foot in front of the other again.

Jennie had been right. He'd needed this.

He was five hundred miles away from his problems, and from this distance he hoped he might find some perspective.

So, for the next few days, whether he tramped through springy glens in the rain, or pushed his way through mist on a hillside, or stood on a summit in a rare moment of sunshine, he let the solitude and the quiet—the soft healing colours—soak into him.

He realised that after Becky had deserted him his mission to protect the world had silently changed into protecting himself. He'd believed he could make himself invincible, believed he could get away with ignoring it all.

So as he climbed he opened the door in the back of his head and looked for monsters. They were real, all right, but not nearly as big and scary as he'd thought they'd be—anger at Becky for leaving him, rage because she'd never told him about Mollie. She'd stolen three years of his daughter's life from him and he couldn't even shout at her for it! Just this thought had left him silent with fury for hours. But there was also guilt, sadness, fear. And, as he took them out, one by one, and shone his torch on them, they all vanished into monster dust.

So, while Alex was physically always on the move, inside he found the stillness he'd been searching for. Alex wasn't a man who needed to weep or shout or punch things to access his emotions. All he needed to do was to stay still long enough for them to catch up with him.

Jennie hated the silence in the house. Mollie had gone to visit Alex's parents for the weekend, and she'd been here alone too many hours. Alex had been gone for six days and was due home tomorrow afternoon, not long before Mollie's grandparents returned her. She knew it had been her idea to set her husband free and send him off to the Highlands for a week, but she hadn't factored in how difficult it would be to be left behind. Waiting. Wondering. Endlessly dissecting every conversation they'd ever had. It was driving her nuts.

She threw down the magazine she'd been reading and hauled herself out of her bubble bath. Even this hadn't managed to calm her down. It was odd. Although she was a city girl, more used to heels than green wellies, what she really wanted to do was go for a bracing walk in the fresh country air. She wrapped a towel around herself and peeked out of the window.

It was overcast, and they'd had nothing but rain for the last few days, but the weather lady on the breakfast news had said it was going to brighten up later.

She got dressed and then went downstairs and grabbed her cardigan off the hook by the back door and plunged her feet into her bright pink flowery wellington boots. Boring old goose-poop green? Not on your life. She might be adapting to life in a village, but she wasn't ready for ugly footwear just yet.

There were plenty of other walkers out this fine Saturday afternoon, but it wasn't long before Jennie lost her sense of camaraderie and got irritated with them. What had happened? Had the whole of south-east London decided to leave suburban bliss to tramp down country lanes? The footpath was heaving with them—muddy dogs bounding backwards and forward, children screaming in delight or whining about how far they were walking. Parents who just didn't seem to care about either. And she could tell they weren't locals because their wellies were just as garish as hers.

Of course, the pub was packed with them, too. Not a table to be had, unless she wanted to wait forty minutes. Which she didn't. So she gave up on the idea of a Caesar salad and a nice glass of wine and headed for home, but on her way she passed the little church on the edge of the Elmhurst estate. She stopped outside the lychgate and looked up the path to the carved oak doors. They were closed, and she had no idea if they'd be locked on a Saturday, but she'd felt strangely serene last time she'd sat on one of those pews. Perhaps it would work again, and at least she'd be alone in there.

The vicar must be a trusting sort because she found the heavy doors swung open when she pushed them. She closed them behind her, not wanting to give any of the tourists any ideas, and then slowly walked down the aisle, careful not to let her boots squeak too loudly on the flagstones, and chose a pew not far from the back. One with a pillar to lean against.

It was cool but not chilly inside the church. Jennie rested against the pillar, listening to her own breath. The gap between *in* and *out* became longer and longer, and soon she felt better, slightly less frazzled. They should bottle the air in this place. It was good stuff.

After a while she decided it might be rude to sit here in complete silence.

I'm back again. Nice place you've got here...

Small talk? Surely she could do better than that. She was famed across London for her witty banter. Only...being cheeky didn't seem right either. She sat still for a moment.

Honesty. Now she remembered. This was the place for that.

I need another favour, she said silently. *I wouldn't ask if it was just for me but, you see, it's for Mollie, too... I chose him last time I sat here. I just need him to choose me back. Do you think that's possible?*

Nothing happened. No sunbeam streamed through a stained glass window. No cherubic fanfare burst the silence, but deep down inside, in a place Jennie hardly knew she had, something came to rest. She sat there for ages, just enjoying the feeling, letting it wash over her, not in big crashing waves; the sensation was similar to the frothy surf that tickled the beach. Soft and rhythmic and soothing.

When she'd drunk her fill of the peace, she stood slowly, walked to the front of the church and stopped right in front of the altar. She tipped her head back to look at the ceiling, got lost in the patterns of the vaulting for a while, and then she turned her head to look back up the aisle.

So different from where she'd said her vows to Alex. It all seemed silly now—eloping to Vegas in an almighty rush. Getting married in a glitzy little chapel by a man in rhinestone-studded ministers' robes, whose teeth were a couple of shades too white. She could have done without the mini-skirted angel as ring-bearer, too.

She turned to face the altar. None of that seemed serious enough to match up to what she and Alex had been through, what they were still facing. But she hadn't understood then how hard marriage could be. In her mind it had all been diamonds and confetti.

But that was just the wedding.

What happened the day after was the true test of the vows. And the day after that. And the day after that. She closed her eyes to stop the sudden stinging. She wanted the *day after that* to keep coming with Alex. She didn't want them to stop. Please, please, if he could just feel the same way.

It might have been in less than solemn surroundings, but she'd meant the promises she'd made him with all of her heart. They, at least, had been unadorned, no glitz to make them seem better than they really were.

The tears had just started to fall in earnest when she heard one of the heavy doors moan. No doubt it was one of those fancy-wellied hikers who'd come to have a nose. Why couldn't they just leave her alone?

She swiped the tears away. Maybe she could bypass them by moving swiftly down the side aisle and be out of the door before anyone had guessed she'd been crying. She lifted her head to check her exit path and froze.

She recognised that silhouette, knew it by heart.

It was Alex.

What was he doing here? How had he found her? He wasn't supposed to be back in Elmhurst until tomorrow.

She'd got used to the dim church interior and the bright light flooding in around him made it impossible to see his face, let alone read his features. She turned to face him fully, begging him with her eyes to just get it over and done with, to deliver her fate.

And then the room was moving, shrinking as Alex got closer and closer. No... It was Alex who was moving. *Running*. It should have only been a few seconds before he reached her, but somehow it took much longer, and as he got closer she started to see his face more clearly.

He was looking at her. Only at her.

No longer wearing that blank mask she'd become accustomed to. His eyes were full of fire and determination and…

That was when he went out of focus, all blurry behind a curtain of tears, but it didn't matter. She'd remember that look for the rest of her life. It was her Alex. And he was running *back* to her.

He pulled her into his arms so hard it was almost a collision. She didn't care. This was where she'd wanted to be, what she'd waited for. She heard herself laughing a long way away, and then the sound stopped, cut off by Alex's lips.

Some time later he whispered something in her ear. Jennie didn't catch it. She was too happy to bother to make sense of mere sounds. When she didn't reply he tried again.

'Jennie…? Will you marry me?'

The clouds of bliss parted enough for her to pull back a little and frown at him. 'Huh?'

Alex smiled at her and she almost forgot to hold on to that thought. He had such a wonderful smile, and it had been missing for such a long time.

'But…we're already married, you dummy.'

Alex just laughed. 'Is that a yes?'

'I…but…but…'

He wrapped himself around her. 'Let's do it again. Here, if you like.'

'W-why? I don't need it, Alex.' She reached out and touched his lips, explored them with her fingertips. 'All I want is you.'

His expression became serious. 'That's why I want to do it properly this time. Not on a whim, but knowing what we want, with our eyes open to all we've been through and all we've yet to face. And I want *you*, Jennie. Always.'

Everything went fuzzy again.

'I've been such a fool,' he muttered.

Jennie swiped her eyes again. 'But you're *my* fool. And you mustn't beat yourself up about it, Mr Perfectionist. You just needed to let yourself grieve for what life threw at you. No one could have held on longer, or been stronger, but even the most invincible of us couldn't have endured what you did without getting wounded along the way.'

He looked off behind her shoulder, then fixed

his gaze on her face again. 'The funny thing is, once I did what you said, once I stared it all eyeball to eyeball, even though it was the hardest thing I've ever done, I found a sense of peace. Nothing worse could happen—except for losing you. I finally saw what I had and what I was about to crush, and I couldn't wait any longer. I had to come and find you.'

She frowned slightly. 'How *did* you find me in here?'

He smiled and gave a little shrug. 'I asked at the pub and someone said they'd seen you come in here. Can't hide anything in a village this size.' He looked around, up at the high ceiling and then back at her. 'Do you want to renew our vows here? It's a lovely place.'

Nice place you have here…

Jennie started to laugh.

That was quick! Thank you!

'What's funny?' Alex said, slightly perplexed.

Jennie just grabbed him and pulled her face close to his. 'I love you,' she murmured, still feeling the joy welling inside her. And Alex replied in kind, although he didn't need words to do it.

EPILOGUE

STEP, together. Step, together. Mollie floated down the aisle just as she'd been shown. It was harder work than she'd thought it would be, because she kept getting excited and going too fast and then almost stepping on the edge of Jennie's lovely white dress.

Jennie looked like a princess, with her hair all up and that thing… What was it called? A tia… A ti…. Well, that sparkly crown-thing in her hair. Her dress was long and smooth and white, and Mollie had decided she wanted one just like it if she ever got married or became a princess. Although, maybe she'd make sure there were more diamonds and pearls on hers. Jennie's was pretty, but it was a bit plain. Not a frill or a bow in sight.

And Daddy almost looked like a prince in his dark suit. He certainly looked very solemn. It was just as well princes didn't wear sparkly crown-things, because it would have looked silly on him. She bit back a giggle and brought her bouquet up higher to cover her mouth.

She still didn't quite understand why Daddy and Jennie needed to get married twice. Hadn't it worked properly the first time? Still, she didn't really mind. She got to wear this lovely white dress with the dark green sash, and got to carry flowers, and everybody she passed as she walked down the aisle behind Daddy and Jennie made a face that told her she looked cute. She pretended not to notice, but secretly she was rather pleased.

The only thing she was sad about was that Mummy wasn't here to see her. She'd heard Daddy say something once about ups and downs and how the mountains had helped him when he felt sad.

They'd stopped at the front of the church now and the vicar person was saying something boring in his up-and-down voice, so Mollie thought a little bit more about mountains. There weren't any in Elmhurst, but maybe, when she was sad, she could climb up to the top of the climbing frame in the garden. That was very tall. She still got sad and cross sometimes, even though she wasn't always sure why, but Jennie had said that was okay, and when she felt like that Jennie would give her a big hug and Daddy would sit down on the floor in the living room with her and they'd play games and read books. She bit her lip. Maybe she wouldn't need the climbing frame after all.

Everyone was singing now, so Mollie took a chance to look behind her. She could see her new friends waving at her from somewhere near the back. She wanted to wave back, but she wasn't sure bridesmaids were allowed to do that, so she just smiled.

The singing stopped and Daddy and Jennie were looking at each other and saying mushy things. Jennie was crying a little bit, so Mollie dug into the secret pocket in her skirt and handed her the hankie Granny Marion had made her put in there earlier.

Everybody laughed. Everybody. The whole church!

She hadn't done anything funny, had she? Daddy was laughing, too, and he scooped her up in his arms and held her close as he and Jennie finished being mushy. Everyone was looking at her.

And then the vicar said Jennie and Daddy could

kiss, so Mollie wriggled out of Daddy's arms and got out of the way before they started getting sloppy. She pulled a face as they started kissing. Yuck!

Everyone laughed again.

Mollie pouted and held her chin high in the air. Some people just didn't get it. Weddings were serious things. She sneaked a look at Daddy and Jennie.

Yup. Still kissing. It seemed they were taking it *very* seriously.

0511 Rom I.P

MILLS & BOON PUBLISH EIGHT LARGE PRINT TITLES A MONTH. THESE ARE THE TITLES FOR JUNE 2011.

FLORA'S DEFIANCE
Lynne Graham

THE RELUCTANT DUKE
Carole Mortimer

THE WEDDING CHARADE
Melanie Milburne

THE DEVIL WEARS KOLOVSKY
Carol Marinelli

THE NANNY AND THE CEO
Rebecca Winters

FRIENDS TO FOREVER
Nikki Logan

THREE WEDDINGS AND A BABY
Fiona Harper

THE LAST SUMMER OF BEING SINGLE
Nina Harrington

MILLS & BOON PUBLISH EIGHT LARGE PRINT TITLES A MONTH. THESE ARE THE TITLES FOR JULY 2011.

A STORMY SPANISH SUMMER
Penny Jordan

TAMING THE LAST ST CLAIRE
Carole Mortimer

NOT A MARRYING MAN
Miranda Lee

THE FAR SIDE OF PARADISE
Robyn Donald

THE BABY SWAP MIRACLE
Caroline Anderson

EXPECTING ROYAL TWINS!
Melissa McClone

TO DANCE WITH A PRINCE
Cara Colter

MOLLY COOPER'S DREAM DATE
Barbara Hannay

Discover Pure Reading Pleasure with

Visit the Mills & Boon website for all the latest in romance

Buy all the latest releases, backlist and eBooks

Find out more about our authors and their books

Join our community and chat to authors and other readers

Free online reads from your favourite authors

Win with our fantastic online competitions

Sign up for our free monthly eNewsletter

Tell us what you think by signing up to our reader panel

Rate and review books with our star system

www.millsandboon.co.uk

 Follow us at twitter.com/millsandboonuk

 Become a fan at facebook.com/romancehq